RC

THE WEREWOLF

A SUPERNATURAL SOCIETY NOVELLA

ROMANCING
THE
WEREWOLF

A SUPERNATURAL SOCIETY
NOVELLA

GAIL CARRIGER

GAIL CARRIGER LLC

GAIL CARRIGER, LLC

ACKNOWLEDGEMENTS

With grateful thanks to my awesome team of beta readers – Amber, Chanie, Dana, Marie, and Tanya. Their charming commentary and helpful tips kept me sane (and my readers free of in-world continuity issues).

A Note on Chronology

The Supernatural Society Novellas can be read in any order.

This particular story is set in the winter of 1895. It follows events chronicled in *Imprudence* and ties romantically to events in *Timeless*.

PROLOGUE

A Timeless Memory

April 1876

Every part of him hurt. It had been a long and vicious fight, the two of them – a Beta and a newly minted werewolf pup, trying to keep an Alpha alive. Trying to keep Lady Kingair from killing them all in her wild lust for revenge. They'd managed it. They'd made it through the night with everyone still relatively intact.

Professor Lyall shuddered over the memory. No clean hits or playfulness in that battle. Biffy had come to his rescue because he could not have taken her on alone. He was a Beta, and Lady Kingair a true Alpha. No contest – he would have died. Except for Biffy. Biffy, so young, barely a werewolf, a baby in their world and innocent of all wrongdoing. He'd come to share the burden of Lady Kingair's righteous anger. He and Lyall had swapped taking her hits, one after another all night long, so the fight remained fair, so they could all survive.

Lyall was bloodied and bruised. Breathing hurt, which meant a few ribs were broken. But he was a werewolf, and he would heal overnight as he slept. Physically, they would all be fine after a day of rest.

Mentally, though?

Lyall felt the burden of embarrassment as well as pain because Biffy knew now. Biffy knew everything. Every messy, degrading, disgusting detail of what life had been like under Alpha Lord Vulkasin Woolsey.

Servicing Lord Vulkasin as Beta near the end had been humiliating nearly beyond bearing. Professor Lyall was hundreds of years old. He'd survived because he knew suffering was finite. But immortality also made time more mutable – it had been a very long five years indeed. He remembered too much of them. Vulkasin, mad with Alpha's curse, turned time longer by doling out pain and humiliation. Since Lady Kingair deserved the truth, Lyall spoke of it in flat, informative tones and tried not to notice Biffy crying. No doubt he wished that he did not have to hear it.

Truth had not saved them from fighting. A different kind of clean hurt, an exorcism all on its own, that Lyall might have, oddly, needed. He had learned to live with the guilt – to protect himself and his pack, he'd arranged for his own Alpha to be slaughtered. He'd destroyed the lives of others in that process, not the least being Lady Kingair and her pack. Had one night of battle purged that? A little. They were, after all, werewolves.

Biffy had come to save him, and so, youth got caught up in the past. But they had survived Lady Kingair's hurt and hurting, and Lyall's own memories. Together, they had survived.

The carriage pulled up before the pack's townhouse. Lyall and Biffy stumbled out, leaning on each other, wrapped in blankets and nothing else. The butler, bless him, met them with coin for the driver and a large, frilly parasol. They made it inside with very little sun damage and a driver's silence purchased outright.

Up the stairs and on to their own separate rooms, Lyall was struck by Biffy's unselfish support. That Biffy had come for him, to help him, only a Beta. Lyall hadn't words to express his gratitude, but he desperately wanted to say something. To do something.

Perhaps some of that desperation showed on his face. Or some of the need. Or some of the loneliness.

Because Biffy said, face drawn with exhaustion, blue eyes calm and kind, "Would you like company, Professor?"

Lyall struggled. "I wouldn't... that is... I couldn't... that is... I'm not all that... capable." He gave a weak hand flap indicating his still-wounded state, his fatigue, and his disheveled appearance all in one.

Biffy gave a little puff of a chuckle. "Only company. I should never presume, even if we were both in perfect health." Self-consciously, he touched his hair, messy from battle and shift. Dandy to the very end.

Lyall barely stopped himself from smiling. *My, but I really am tired.* He schooled his features, reaching for backbone and untapped strength. *I haven't much of that left.*

He couldn't take advantage. "Pity, pup? Now that you know what Lord Woolsey did to me? It was a long time ago."

Biffy tilted his head, showing his neck submissively. "No, sir. Never that. Respect, I suppose. To survive such things and still be sane."

How does he always know exactly the right thing to say?

They were interrupted, at that moment, by the butler checking in on them. It wasn't odd, in a werewolf house, to find two bloodied men talking politely in the upstairs hallway. But it was odd to find them lingering there after sunrise. The butler was understandably confused. Lyall sent him on his way with polite excuses.

Biffy turned to make his way to his own sleeping chamber. His shoulders were slumped even further, rejection on top of exhaustion.

Lyall could not bear it.

He placed a hand on Biffy's arm. He tilted his head in silent invitation and opened the door to his own quarters. Biffy hesitated. Lyall wondered if he had misread the signs. His own shoulders curved slightly, and he moved into his room, alone, glancing back only once.

To see Biffy give one of his glorious quiet smiles and follow.

They climbed into Lyall's small bed, good for nothing more than sleep. But sleeping together was more than Lyall had ever hoped for.

They awoke after sunset, entwined and naked. By mutual assent, they touched each other then, careful kisses and soft caresses. They were both physically recovered from their ordeal, but remembered injuries made them reverent. Lyall could not stop running his fingers through Biffy's hair. Before, when he was human, those dark curls had been coifed, tamed, and set. Now that he was a werewolf, they were silken and wild. No doubt this distressed Biffy, but Lyall adored it.

Biffy was tender with him and not ashamed. He took charge, building everything between them into insistence and yearning. He was young enough for Lyall to be surprised by his knowledge and his skill with tongue, and fingers, and oil. They took their time with each other, and there was no question that it was Lyall who wanted claiming. Who needed the dark spike and slide of knowing that he was desired. Biffy was intent but never forceful. Perhaps his movements were gentled by the memory of what Lyall had suffered in the past, or perhaps it was simply his way. To be in control but kind with it, to use dominance as a way of focusing on Lyall's pleasure first.

It was oddly sweet, and oddly glorious, and so very, very necessary.

When Biffy lay, flush against him, Lyall nuzzled into his neck. They fit well together, neither of them very big for werewolves.

Biffy said, tones smooth, "You truly intend to leave and become Kingair's Beta, even after all you sacrificed for this pack?"

"I must make amends." Lyall did not stop his nuzzling.

"So far away from London?"

That brought a new pain. Lyall had known some of what was coming. This was his real pack. London was his home. He would be leaving both, and now he would be leaving Biffy, too. But he would make right what he had done to Lady Kingair, and that meant submitting himself to her will and her stewardship. "It won't be forever."

They spoke of other things then – pack politics, government position, other kinds of necessity. Lyall could only hope that Biffy understood. He wasn't really leaving them so much as going *to* something vital, for a time.

Eventually, Biffy worked up the courage to ask, "Will

you come back here after?"

"I will try." *I will arrange everything. I will plan it out, and I will fix it all, and this time around, no one will have to die.*

CHAPTER ONE

The Problem with Purple

December 1895

"But Alpha, purple is simply not appropriate." Quinn's growly voice somehow edged into whining.

The rest of the werewolf pack tried to shush him, but the damage was done.

"I *beg* your pardon!" Sandalio de Rabiffano, newly minted Lord Falmouth, better known to the rarified fuzz and fang of the supernatural set as Biffy, Alpha of the London Pack, nearly leapt to his feet... at the dinner table. He was *that* offended. Of course, he remembered himself long before he could commit such a profound breach of etiquette. He was, after all, still Biffy.

He narrowed his eyes instead. "I assure you, purple is a perfectly delightful color and is more than appropriate to all venues, ages, genders, and species!"

"It doesn't hearken to nature," Phelan came to his pack mate's defense with an intellectual argument. He cocked his head socratically, his studied air rather defeated by the fact that he had to stop stuffing his face with steak and kidney pie in order to talk. Biffy swung his discerning glare onto him, judging his manner, his decision to speak against his Alpha, his choice of argument, and his ill-judged belief that Quinn had opened the floodgates of objection.

This anti-purple rhetoric would be nipped, most sharply, in the bud. "Plenty of lovely natural things are purple: sunsets, sunrises for that matter, iris, aubergines, oysters." Nip nip nip! "Although" – he frowned, and then remembered he didn't like the way this wrinkled his forehead, so stopped – "these are all different *shades* of purple. Is that the true objection? Should I choose a different shade?"

A chorus of groans met that. They'd already been at this for an hour, Biffy finally settling on this particular deep, rich, dark plum velvet. Ordinarily, the pack didn't care about interior decorations and would rather he choose without involving them. Ordinarily, he would have. But this was a communal curtain situation and they were his pack. Curtains should *matter* to his pack. And now, it seemed, of a sudden they did matter.

Biffy pursed his lips. He *knew* this was the correct color. Knew it in his very bones. Bones that moved and shifted and broke every full moon, so possibly not as reliable as they might once have been, but still... "Why are you arguing with me on this particular detail? Purple would suit the room best. You never usually care two tail shakes for this sort of thing." *Why object now about something I know is right?*

Adelphus, who was at that moment wearing a purple evening jacket (not plum, more violet, but still), looked monumentally uncomfortable. He fiddled with one of the fabric samples set out before them. Biffy suppressed the instinct to slap the man's hand away – Adelphus might leave a grease stain. But no, it was fine, Adelphus was mostly tame. "I simply feel the green..."

"In that room? Are you mad?" Biffy tried not to let the frustration color his voice. He knew what he was talking about. This was what he did. He made rooms beautiful. He made people beautiful. Or he used to, before he lost most of his soul and creativity.

Doubt, his old friend, shook him then. *Maybe I'm wrong. Maybe the purple is unpleasant. Maybe I've lost my eye for color as well as everything else. No. Stop second-guessing. It's the purple or nothing.* And nothing was not an option in a house full of werewolves. Sunlight being rather more of an issue when one was allergic to it.

He took a breath. *I'm the Alpha, for goodness' sake. Aren't they supposed to listen to me? Instinctively obey me?*

"God's teeth, it's only curtains!" Even Rafe, the most easygoing of the pack, was getting annoyed.

Biffy huffed. "Curtains," he explained slowly as though to a very thick child (which, to be fair, rather defined Rafe's character), "are a *serious* business."

"Don't you think they'll be too dark for the room?" Hemming was clearly not at all sure of himself. It sounded as if he were trying to come up with an excuse. As if he really had some other reason for objecting. As if they all did.

What is going on here?

Biffy swept a critical gaze over his nervous pack. "All right, chaps, what's the truth here? What's actually wrong with purple?"

His pack all looked collectively guilty. They exchanged glances. Finally, they all turned to Adelphus as if he were the one best at calming their new, young, purple-minded Alpha.

Poor Adelphus. He isn't my Beta, but he keeps getting cast in that role. Biffy winced away from that thought, like touching a sore tooth. He didn't want to think about his Beta. He didn't want to miss him.

He'd agree with me about the purple.

A nice dark plum, ideal to show off the daring ash furniture and sumptuous cream brocades he'd chosen for the rest of the drawing room. With some luscious ferns scattered about, and a few other plants, shelves of books, and other knickknacks. It would look rich and striking yet bright and welcoming and...

Adelphus looked uncomfortable. *But at least he's stylish. Perhaps I should listen to him. We have something in common.*

Biffy paused to think a little on that. It took a great deal of effort for a werewolf to have style. Getting naked once a month, ripping clothes constantly, and turning into a slavering beast was only the start of the afterlife's many dandy challenges.

Something for me to be proud of. Biffy had come a long way from the lonely, scruffy want-to-be vampire of his first few years as a werewolf pup. *My hair alone was a complete shambles.* Certainly, he still wasn't a very good Alpha. He'd no idea how to run a pack. He'd never successfully metamorphosed a claviger, and he was still looked down upon by other Alphas. In fact, the litany of his failings over the past twenty years since his metamorphosis filled his brain, but... *At least I am a werewolf with style. And I can bloody well pick out curtains!*

He fully glared at Adelphus, putting Alpha will

behind the look.

Adelphus crumpled. "See here, Alpha. I mean no disrespect and no insult to your former life." His eyes were wary.

"Go on," said Biffy, trying not to let his voice sink into a growl.

"But, sir..."

Now that felt weird. Adelphus was at least a hundred years his senior, possibly twice that, and *sir* was an honorific Biffy did not feel he deserved.

"Yes?"

"Purple is a vampire color."

Biffy let out a long sighing kind of snort. "Oh, for goodness' sake! We have colors now?"

Quinn tried to help. "It's accepted all 'round as standard practice for spaces and coaches and cushions and that sort of thing." He failed the dismount.

"That sort of *thing*?" Biffy let his outrage show.

"It's only, Alpha, this is a big step, us moving away from Himself next door. We don't want any reminders of previous intimacies." Hemming was trying to be kind.

What he was saying was actually: *We don't want* you *to have any reminders*.

Biffy suddenly understood. They were worried he was pining for lost futures. How sweet of them.

"How many times do I have to tell you I'm not upset about being a werewolf instead of a vampire?"

Incredulous looks all 'round.

"Fine, I'm not upset *anymore*. Honestly."

All the werewolves were displaying varying degrees of disbelief. Biffy had made no secret, at first, that werewolf was not what he wanted for an afterlife. Back then, it had been hard to hide, he was so wounded, knowing he could have made it. To have enough excess soul to become a werewolf meant he might have become a vampire instead. Vampire would have suited him so much better – his personality, his plans, his future, his soul (or what was left of it). But that wasn't what happened, and he'd had twenty years to come to terms with that. Purple curtains were not going to sway him into flights of his former melancholy.

I assure you, he wanted to say again, *I'm not pining!* Except that he was. Only it wasn't for a state of undead – it was for a person. It wasn't so much an ache, a void at the edge of his consciousness, as a missing piece. The same piece that was missing from his pack, the balance point that they all yearned for. The one who could, so easily and gently, have settled the matter of purple curtains.

Biffy told himself for the millionth time that it was nothing more than an Alpha's need for his Beta. He refused to believe that after twenty years, his heart hurt for a connection it had had so long ago, for such a short space of time. He forced his mind not to go in that direction. There were too many other things, too many important things that he must deal with, and pining for his Beta (non-sexually or otherwise) wouldn't solve anything.

With a sigh, he capitulated. Which likely wasn't a good decision. Alphas were supposed to be strong, commanding, hold to their point of view. Or something like that.

He went with his second option. "I suppose blood red is out, too."

The pack all looked at one another.

"We werewolves customarily get outdoor colors like

browns and greens and such." Phelan was trying to help.

Biffy glared. "I am attempting to give us an aura of sophistication! It's 1895. We live in London. Earth tones are so very last decade!"

The werewolves now looked as though they were trying not to laugh. At least a few of them did.

"Why do vampires get to have purple? Is it a rule? Something to do with royalty?" Biffy had learned there were lots of unwritten rules to immortality. The werewolves called them *protocols*, but really they were traditionally codified rules.

Adelphus smiled. "Not officially. It's more to do with Rome."

Biffy grinned back. "Oh, yes, ancient history, is it?"

Biffy knew he had a bit of a lax attitude about tradition. But then again, wasn't that part of his role? In his lucid days, before the previous Alpha went mad with Alpha's curse, Lord Maccon would say, *This is your time, Biffy. Bring us into the modern age. We have to learn to accommodate the present, or we are going to become obsolete. You're important to all werewolves – you represent a new kind of Alpha.*

I'm failing. I'm failing him. And I'm failing them. Well, us, I suppose I should say. He looked at his pack sitting around the dinner table, worried, uncomfortable.

Biffy stood. He wasn't particularly tall, but he had good form and excellent posture. He was a practiced gentleman and he called upon that sophistication (in lieu of arrogance) so that he could put his beautifully shod foot very firmly down.

"Purple curtains. End of discussion."

Adelphus opened his mouth. Biffy glared. "End. Of. Discussion."

Adelphus snapped his mouth closed and tilted his head quickly to show his neck. "Yes, Alpha."

With a start, the others followed suit.

Biffy marched from the room. Feeling a little faint. Which he attributed to not having had time to eat – too busy arguing about curtains.

Biffy had elected to move the pack – his pack – for various reasons. But the main one was standing in the house next door's entranceway, entreating him to come visit as he stormed past in a purple-curtain temper. Biffy was on a mission to settle his nerves. His authority had been questioned, not as Alpha but as arbiter of good taste. It made him feel unstable and petulant. Which was a long way of saying – he had hats to decorate. Having a gossip with his former lover, ex vampire-master, inveterate scandalmonger, and next-door neighbor was nowhere near as restful as hat decorating.

But Lord Akeldama was nothing if not persuasive, and Biffy was nothing if not courteous.

He might, of course, have pretended not to hear. But he had supernatural hearing, and Lord Akeldama knew that.

"Biffy! *Pudding!* Come be social with your old chum, it's perishingly dull right now."

It was also perishingly cold. Not as bad as last year when the blasted Thames had become an ice pit, but London was having another frigid winter in a string of them. Lord Akeldama, however, stood defiantly in his doorway wearing little more than a charming silk smoking jacket (though he didn't smoke), a precocious gold monocle (although he had perfect vision), and skin-tight satin trousers (although it was not yet visiting hours). Vampires did not really feel the cold. They were cold already.

Biffy sighed, admiring the trousers. He no longer wore anything so well fitted. It was too difficult to strip out of tight clothing with speed and finesse. He shouldn't have been shocked to learn (although he had been) that werewolves got naked a great deal more frequently than anyone else.

He admired the consequences of course – Biffy was a great appreciator of the male physique, and werewolves mainly came big and muscled. While that wasn't his particular romantic preference, he could still admire – on an intellectual level, of course. But he did miss tight clothing. He himself had a slender build, but with nice lean muscles that he'd taken care to maintain, even in his human dandy lifetime, with fencing and dancing. He'd once quite enjoyed showing himself off with fashion. To be frank, he missed tight trousers.

"Are you admiring the cut of my jib, dahling?" inquired the vampire, tapping his monocle and smiling – without showing fang.

Biffy paused on the threshold and gave Lord Akeldama an assessing look. *Goodness, I miss flirting.*

"Will you be hoisting a petard any time soon?"

Lord Akeldama laughed. "Shall I run it up the flagpole and see if anything salutes?" His eyes drifted downwards, speculatively.

Biffy allowed a gentle chuckle to leak forth.

Lord Akeldama stepped back and gestured for him to come inside.

"Am I welcome?" Biffy hesitated.

"Ah, *dear boy*, you've been studying vampire-werewolf relationship protocols again, haven't you?"

"I must learn."

"Of course you must. Please, my *lovely*, come inside, do."

At an outright verbalized invitation, Biffy walked inside the vampire's home.

He was hit with a pang of regret almost instantly. Very little had changed. The hallway was still overly decorated in a French rococo style, full of opulence, gilt, and seductive tapestries featuring shepherds in compromising positions. There were marble statues of cupids and thick Persian rugs. Certainly, it wasn't to Biffy's taste, but it was to *taste*. It had a point of view and Biffy admired that in a house. And it was achingly familiar. *I lived here for half as much time as I lived with the pack next door, and yet I miss this place more. Sentimentality? Perhaps it's simply that I was so very happy here.*

Lord Akeldama led him into his luxurious drawing room. Not the more comfortable sitting room – that was reserved for family and Biffy was no longer family.

"Tea? Pink slurp? Something raw and still wiggling?"

Biffy smiled. "A slurp would be lovely." It wasn't to his taste, but courtesy must take preeminence with vampires, even ex-lovers and old friends – especially then.

Lord Akeldama whistled up his current favorite drone, a beautiful young man with raven hair and catlike black eyes named Winkle. *Well, not named Winkle, but called Winkle by my lord, and thus everyone else.*

"Winkle, *darling*. Two pink slurps when you have a moment."

"Of course, my lord, coming right up."

"And we are *not* to be disturbed."

Winkle frowned, looking disturbed himself. "Oh, but sir..."

"What is it, my pet?"

"There's the matter of the kitten?"

"Kitten, Winkle?"

"Yes, sir, you promised Kippers. Remember? You agreed that we should get a new kitten, since Madame Pudgemuffin..."

Lord Akeldama tapped his lip with one fingertip. "Yes, I did, didn't I? Is Kippers bringing around the candidate soonish?"

"They're in the kitchen as we speak."

"They? *They!* I believe I was quite clear on this matter – only *one* cat at a time in this household. I can't be seen to have more than one cat, it simply isn't done. It's too much. Too eccentric in a vampire."

Biffy leaned back. Trying not to slide comfortably into the ridiculous banter of Lord Akeldama's household. Trying not to enjoy the conversation too much. Trying not to jump in and mediate, as once would have been his role. It hurt. By George, it hurt. Although not as much as it once had. Twenty years were remarkably numbing.

"But sir! They are so cute. A brother-and-sister pair."

Lord Akeldama frowned. "Do they match to my aesthetic?"

"A ginger and a tabby, sir."

Lord Akeldama winced. "I shall have to entirely redecorate the sitting room. Ginger indeed!"

"He has the cutest little face..." Winkle gave a winning smile. "Looks like he's got a most serious statement mustache."

"Mustache? Mustache! In my house?" Lord Akeldama was not to be persuaded by mustaches on cats. Or anyone else, for that matter.

Winkle made his eyes big. "Please, sir?"

Lord Akeldama gave a very elegant snort. "I shall *think* about it. Now, bring us the slurps and leave us be for twenty minutes. I trust you can entertain the candidates until then? How many of you are home at the moment?"

"Only four of us drones, my lord."

"That should be enough for two kittens."

More fateful words were never spoken. Biffy hid a grin.

Winkle nodded. "I hope so, sir. They are most ebullient."

"Well, you'd best hop to it, then, hadn't you, *my sweet*?"

Winkle hurried off, returning in mere moments with the champagne mixed with blood, and then excusing himself with a slightly panicked look in his eye.

Lord Akeldama sipped his slurp and turned his piercing eyes back to Biffy.

"So, Alpha, how is everything with your new pack?"

"As well as can be expected."

"It has only been a few months since you became the power behind the fur. Is that correct? You know me and time."

Biffy could have calculated to the exact hour he'd assumed leadership of the London Pack, but he didn't want to let his former master know how much the responsibility weighed upon him. "A few, as you say, my lord."

"None of *that* anymore, my dear. We're equals now."

Biffy winced. Technically, of course, he was Lord Akeldama's social superior. An Alpha werewolf with a full pack outranked a rove vampire. He'd recently been learning all about it. He didn't think Lord Akeldama would like it if he mentioned that little fact.

Lord Akeldama put down his drink softly. "A little bird told me you'll be leaving us soon."

Biffy wasn't surprised at all by the knowledge, although he was a little shocked by the seriousness of the accusation. Lord Akeldama was never serious.

"Yes." He made the excuses in his head because it would never do to volunteer information to a vampire, least of all Lord Akeldama – not anymore. *I don't think it's healthy for werewolves to be in such close proximity to a vampire. I need my own space, to establish a change from one Alpha to the next. I need change. And I need to redecorate.*

"Sweetie, I think it's a *wonderful* idea."

"You do?" Biffy blinked at him.

"You're taking into account established influence of the supernatural set in other parts of the city? We're a bit weighted at this juncture to north and west London."

Biffy fell, too easily, into their old strategic confidences. "Of course."

"Not Dulwich?" Lord Akeldama gave a delicate little shudder. "The name alone."

"Certainly not! Greenwich."

"Ah." The pink drink swirled in the glass as the vampire contemplated the bubbles therein.

"There's Blackheath right there and it's still close enough to the important parts of town." Biffy tried not to sound as if he were defending his decision.

"Not too rough-and-tumble?"

"For me, perhaps, but not for them. In addition, there is the theater and the music hall."

"You're thinking of new clavigers? Very wise, dear boy. Very wise indeed."

Biffy tried not to puff up at the praise from his former master.

"Well, my pet, you will bring some charm and civilizing force to the area."

"That's the general idea, yes." Biffy leaned forward, determined to get them away from this serious track. "How do you feel about purple curtains?"

"What shade of purple?"

"My point exactly!"

And just like that, they were back on familiar ground. Biffy spent a comfortable quarter of an hour debating the measure of interior decorating and the relative advantages when combined with the rather brutish attitude most werewolves extended towards furniture and finally rose to depart.

Cries from the sitting room notwithstanding (the kittens, it seemed, were indeed a handful), it was time for Biffy to take his leave.

"Oh, for goodness' sake, what has their britches in a bunch now?" Lord Akeldama pondered, as he led Biffy towards his inner sanctum rather than the front door.

Biffy hesitated to follow the vampire into his private quarters, but he was wildly curious.

Lord Akeldama pushed open the sitting-room door to chaos. One of his drones was perched precariously atop the back of a settee trying to reach a small ginger fluff-ball that was, apparently, climbing the (not purple) curtains. Another drone was trying to gently shake said kitten off said curtains. The kitten clung as if life and limb depended upon it.

Two other drones were down on their knees (at great risk of indelicate rending, given they took after their vampire master in the matter of tightly fitted trousers). They were fishing about under the self-same settee, presumably for the second kitten. Several chairs had been knocked over and there was a bowl sitting in what could only be a damp patch of spilled milk.

Biffy glanced at Lord Akeldama to assess his reaction to the madness. The vampire's first glance was one of shining affection, but he quickly schooled his features into that of disciplinarian and teacher. Biffy also watched him take in Winkle's pert bottom as he attempted to retrieve the tabby. Or perhaps that hunger was the result of a bit of naked neck (between hair and cravat) exposed by the kneeling drone.

Even as a drone himself, Biffy had never deluded himself about Lord Akeldama. Perhaps there had once been a youthful fantasy about Biffy becoming a vampire and the two of them immortal together forever. But in his heart, Biffy had always known that he was a one-immortal kind of dandy, and Lord Akeldama was not. The vampire had never led him on. Lord Akeldama's love, such as it was, was always transient and shared.

Now Biffy understood why. True, Biffy was a young immortal, but he was almost fifty, and he'd seen his mortal friends grow old while he had not. Or die in the attempt to become like him. He wasn't yet old enough to have grown the protective thickness around his heart, the one that made Lord Akeldama's smiles brittle, but Biffy now knew why it was there. Frankly, he wasn't convinced he'd ever be the type that preferred to share. For now, he'd decided he'd rather be alone than constantly watch his lovers leave him, one way or another. As a drone, Biffy had understood, and had shared, because that was the only way he got a piece of Lord Akeldama. As a werewolf, even if it were possible, he wouldn't take that wager.

I'm on my own now.

Lord Akeldama was distracted, on to the next crisis, on to the next evening's entertainment, on to the next toy. It was how he weathered immortality. *I wonder if he's as lonely in his way as I am in mine.*

Biffy bent and kissed the vampire's cheek, aware of the imposition. Aware of the hairs rising on his arm and the press of his own supernatural instincts urging him to change shape. Protect himself. Instincts that screamed in his head. *Vampire. Predator. Not pack. Enemy.* He was aware too of the faint smell of carrion, like rotting flesh and decayed bones, that hung under the citrus cologne that Lord Akeldama always wore. Something Biffy had never scented when they lived together. When Biffy was human.

"Good-bye, my lord," he said, meaning it this time. Because that smell would always be there now. Because it would be the last time he said "my lord" to any vampire. Because under lost love and changed identities was one ineffable fact more vital than the horror of that smell – every fiber in Biffy's werewolf soul knew he was no servant to this man anymore. And never would be again.

Lord Akeldama looked at him and knew it too, in that perfect-quick way he had. One of the reasons Biffy had loved him so. "Lord Falmouth, best of luck with the relocation. And…" A pause and a slight curl of the lip. "…Greenwich."

Biffy inclined his head. He had a memory then. A brief flash of this man – who managed, somehow, to still be a *man* as well as a vampire – under him. Lean and white and needy. And taken. For back then, in those few hours of privacy, when it was only the two of them, together, Biffy had always been the one to dominate. He had been the one in charge. Those rare moments, among all the rest of his time as a drone, had also been the very best. *I should have known it would never work between us, werewolf or not.*

"Lord Akeldama. Best of luck with the kittens." Biffy let himself out of the vampire's house, breathing in fresh cool air unscented by death, and breathing out a lifetime of regrets.

CHAPTER TWO

Home for the Holidays

Professor Randolph Lyall was tired. Tired from his toes to the tips of the (too long) sandy-colored hair on his (always, despite the length) neat and tidy head. London looked dirty and a little sad, but after so long away, he was still seized with the joy of it. It spread over and in him like bathing in slightly cold, but probably still edible, pea soup. Very cold, as it turned out. And congealed.

Home.

He'd separated from the Kingair Pack at Southampton – passing off his former Alpha to her new Beta. His replacement was there, waiting for her to disembark the ship – as any serviceable Beta should be. Phineas was a good-natured chap, a loner for most of his life, but Beta to the core. He'd need all three traits to put up with Sidheag Maccon, the Lady of Kingair. Still, Phineas was accustomed to Alpha females, if his partner was anything to go by. Lyall didn't know her name – better not to. Those who inquired too closely into the identity of the Wicker Chicken disappeared. How the Dewan would survive henceforth, without his two best intelligencers, was anyone's guess. But Lyall, who dealt all too often with the shadows, was glad to have the Wicker Chicken out of London at last, and Lady Kingair in very capable hands. What Phineas couldn't keep in line, the Wicker Chicken would.

Lyall felt almost happy about such a smooth transfer of pack power. An unusual sensation for him to grapple with. The Kingair Pack, plus new additions, were all looking forward to some quiet time in Scotland. All Lyall needed do was wish them a pleasant farewell, which he did. Surprised to find that he actually meant it, for a change.

Not that he hadn't tried his best to be a good Beta. Lady Kingair deserved nothing less than his best effort. But she hadn't been his Alpha, not really. His real Alpha was here, in London.

Home.

Lyall jumped down from the hackney and paid the driver, eager to see his friends and pack-mates again. And his Alpha. *My Alpha.*

Unfortunately, much to his shock, the pack house was empty. He could smell the absence from the road, no pack present. Hadn't been for a week or more.

Terror hit him hard and sure and sudden to the stomach, instantly coiling it into knots. He'd been at sea. Had he missed the news? Had something happened to his pack?

I left it too long. I knew he needed me back. Bloody hell, what if he couldn't control them without me? What if he failed? What if they had to be eliminated?

His face, however, slid into a mask of cold indifference, and he kept his footsteps measured as he approached the house next door instead.

Lord Akeldama will know what happened. Where they are. Lord Akeldama always knows.

Lyall's knock was answered, after a long pause, by a harried-looking drone. "Oh, good evening? Who are you? Never mind, come in quickly, do, or she'll... nope, there she goes! Quick, catch her!"

Lyall bent down and scooped up the kitten before she had a chance to escape over the threshold – werewolf speed and werewolf reflexes. Like most cats, she'd no interest in objecting to his wolf nature. Prey animals, like sheep and rabbits, always seemed to know that they were likely thought tasty. Even when a werewolf was in his human form. Dogs, of course, liked to challenge or cringe. Cats, however, were simply cats about the whole supernatural thing. Or they had adapted to become so. Lyall had read a fascinating theory once that cats had malleable souls. Or, at the very least, a sense of superiority so strong that they regarded even immortals as their inferiors.

Well, who am I to challenge feline judgment?

The kitten in his arms struggled briefly and then gave him a wide-eyed look of perfect innocence. Finally, when Lyall cuddled her to his chest, she butted against his jaw and issued some consolatory (if raspy) tiny-tongue licks to his chin.

The drone quickly shut the door behind him. "Oh, sir, I am so sorry. Unpardonably rude but she will keep getting out, and she's a bit too young as yet for the streets of London."

Lyall clucked at the kitten and rubbed her cheeks. The kitten began emitting a remarkably loud purr for such a wee little thing.

The drone looked embarrassed. "I shouldn't have

allowed you in like that. This being the house of a vampire and all, and your being a strange chap and unknown element."

Lyall looked the young man up and down. He appeared young and not quite as well dressed as Lyall had come to expect from one of Lord Akeldama's drones. Lyall had been away from London for twenty years, but Lord Akeldama was a vampire and his tastes and standards didn't alter *that* much.

"You're new, I take it?"

"Is it very obvious?"

"Only to the oldest friends, my *dearest* Tiffin!" A cheerful voice spoke from within the drawing room – bright but a little too sharp, like untempered lemon juice.

Lyall knew it well. He also knew the smell; it hadn't changed in the slightest. Citrus and hair wax, and old dead blood, faintly rotten and musty – vampire with a Lord Akeldama twist.

His hackles rose, the wolf ones, buried deep under urbanity and efficiency. He let them rise and then smoothed them over, accustomed to the wave of savagery battling against his human self. The wild predator, all emotions and instincts. It did no good to fight them, so he let them be, simply never let them *show*. A consummate man of culture, he became nothing more or less than Professor Lyall, an old Beta werewolf. Safe. He doubted even Lord Akeldama noticed the tiny twitch of territorial defense that briefly surfaced at the, frankly, disgusting smell of vampire.

I am, after all, in his home. It is on me to behave.

Lord Akeldama approached, looking as well put together and beautiful as ever. He was a paragon of calculated perfection. Lyall wasn't fooled. Charmed –

always – but never fooled.

This was a game they could both play, and play well. "Lord Akeldama, how delightful to see you again and in such good health. You don't look a day over five hundred, if I do say so myself."

"Dolly, darling, you *flatter* me. Just now returned to town and you visit *me* first! To what do I owe the *incalculable* honor?"

Lyall was tired, or he might have been less blunt. He cuddled the kitten and said, over the purr, "I seem to have misplaced my pack. Terribly careless, I know."

Lord Akeldama gave a tinkling little laugh. "Of course, you realize *everyone* expected you a bit sooner."

Lyall hid his wince. He had tried to return right after Biffy took over, but circumstances had not allowed it.

Lord Akeldama assessed him. Those changeable eyes of his were so calculating. Lyall knew what the vampire saw. Lyall had let his sandy hair grow long, and sported a neat beard in response to the current fashions. He wasn't sure why he'd adopted such a marked physical change. But he had. No doubt Lord Akeldama would understand exactly what this implied.

Immortals didn't grow hair, not like normal people, so for Lyall to have changed his, there could be only one explanation. He'd spent months inside the God Breaker Plague zone in Egypt. There, his immortality, and all stasis that went with it, had been broken. He had aged too, although not noticeably. It had been oddly restful and liberating to be mortal again. He had thought to simply... stay. Maybe, finally, to stop.

Except that he wasn't done yet. He had an Alpha to serve. *Another one.* More lives to live.

He wasn't sure what he expected from the vampire. A

snide comment: *How was Egypt?* Or a probing one: *Are the Maccons well?* He got neither.

The vampire allowed his new appearance to pass without remark. A truly out-of-character maneuver.

"I'm afraid, Dolly dear, they up and moved. Abandoned me to my own devices."

Is that relief in Lord Akeldama's tone? "They did?"

"Several weeks ago. At least, I think it was several weeks. You know me and *time*."

"Old bedfellows?"

Lord Akeldama laughed.

Lyall shook his head trying to make sense of this. But why would Biffy leave his love? Neighbors were better than nothing. "But where?" he asked, trying not to sound plaintive.

Lord Akeldama's mouth twisted slightly. "To Greenwich."

Lyall swallowed. He wasn't sure why, but the statement felt like an accusation, as if for some reason Lord Akeldama blamed Lyall for the relocation. Perhaps that accounted for the lack of personal commentary on the state of Lyall's hair. *Anger.*

He let his wolf a little closer to the surface. "Of course, Blackheath. An excellent choice for pack, and it balances out the supernatural distribution over the greater London environs."

"My dear Dolly, that is almost *exactly* what I said about the decision." Lord Akeldama smiled, showing fang. *Definitely anger. Or disappointment.*

Both of us know, of course, that there are a million other reasons for Biffy to move his pack away from you. Did you try to get him back? Did you try to break his heart all over again? Or was it simply too much for both of you, wanting and not being able to have?

Lyall allowed his eyes to flicker over the ancient vampire. Old friend or old nemesis? One never knew with vampires. Lyall was pushing decades, a long afterlife for a werewolf – *I must be at least four hundred at this point.* But Lord Akeldama was pushing centuries. Roves, the ones that did not go mad, could live a very long time indeed.

"Where, exactly?"

"Ah, I wasn't given the courtesy of an address." The vampire pretended to be hurt. As though his drones had not already determined the exact location. It was damn near impossible to hide a pack. Hives were no problem at all, but packs had no subtlety.

"And you don't know?" Lyall would not give him quarter.

"What fun is there in that? Use your much-vaunted werewolf nose, Dolly my sweet."

Lyall sighed. No point in arguing. He inclined his head. The win must go to the vampire this time. *At least I know they're in Greenwich. God, I'm tired.*

Lord Akeldama, for lack of another way of putting it, took pity on him. "However, as we are heading into the Christmas season, you must know where your Alpha is most likely to be on a busy night like tonight."

"Yes, of course. Thank you for that, my lord."

Lord Akeldama dipped his head, a funny, sad movement. "Welcome home, Professor."

"Thank you, sir. Happy Christmas." Lyall, ensuring the kitten was well ensconced in the young, new, confused drone's arms, touched the brim of his hat and strode back out into the cold night.

They'd never even left the foyer.

The relocation had gone relatively smoothly, or as smoothly as such things go with a pack of werewolves. It helped that most of the London Pack was actually in London at the moment. Everyone said that when Alpha transition occurred, a pack was justified in recusing itself from military obligation for at least a decade. Fortunately, the government agreed. In fact, Queen Victoria was so set on the power shift going smoothly with her largest and strongest pack (especially as the last power transfer had resulted in a botched assassination attempt), she'd given the London Pack a fifteen-year dispensation from all foreign service – to ensure cohesion under a new Alpha.

It was still peculiar to Biffy that he had actually met her. *The Queen of England!* She was shorter than he had expected. He'd stood before her while she granted him lands and title, for all Alphas were aristocrats by royal decree.

"We are very pleased," she'd said, looking a little less constipated than usual in her evident pleasure, "to have a city pack at all. We should like to keep it healthy. We understand you to be a most civilized young man." Her eyes had said she approved Biffy's well-coiffed appearance and fine manners. Even at seventy-six, the queen was said to have an eye for pretty men. Biffy was not ashamed to say he preyed upon that weakness. He was the only existing werewolf Alpha who could. Oh, there were other good-looking Alphas in England; they simply weren't *pretty*.

"Arise, my Lord Rabiffano, Earl of Falmouth."

So, now Biffy was a proper earl of something he was

rather embarrassed to say aloud. And he was Alpha of a strong if anti-purple pack. He still preferred to be a milliner. Fortunately, such eccentricity was permitted. Actually, it was permitted even more so now that he was an aristocrat. After all, proper aristocrats always had peculiar hobbies. Of course, by rights he ought to give away his art to the deserving poor. *Engaging in trade* couldn't even be excused as insanity, let alone eccentricity, but Chapeau de Poupe was a thriving business concern, and Biffy liked selling hats. So everyone, including the shopper, turned a blind eye to either his habits or his title, depending on how they felt about it at the moment.

It was a generally accepted practice that when working on milling hats, he was referred to as Mr Rabiffano. When advising on the choice of a hat, he was to be called Lord Falmouth. And when actually handling the expenses, a mere Biffy would suffice. It was odd what society would do to accommodate the acquisition of a really beautiful hat.

He was Lord Falmouth at the moment, taking the clientele in hand, advising the rampaging hordes on the efficaciousness of feathers over flowers for the winter season.

He was avoiding the new pack house. All was still in chaos after the move, and he had learned his own Alpha moods well enough to realize his pack must be left to squabble about who got which room without him. Otherwise, he was compelled to interfere, and in these kinds of petty cohabitation matters, his authority was neither needed nor wanted.

So, he'd taken refuge in his favorite place, where he could bury himself in the beauty of pretty things and the organization of attractive wares.

Until his hard-won calm was disturbed.

He smelled the other werewolf before he saw him. There was a scent of strangeness, wolf but not quite his pack, wild with the spice of dry, hot sands and exotic lands.

Look at me, getting poetical even with a possible fight on my hands. How droll.

It wasn't odd, a loner werewolf in London, but it was for a loner to enter his hat shop uninvited and unannounced. He braced himself, nervous.

Why a challenger right now? As if moving wasn't stressful enough. I suppose he couldn't simply be after a hat, could he? No.

Not that the hat shop wasn't popular. The titillation of the previous owner, a cross-dressing evil genius inventor of exotic tastes, had given over to the titillation of being served by a werewolf and his clavigers. Young ladies flocked to Chapeau de Poupe in record numbers. Mothers and chaperones allowed this because the danger inherent in a werewolf dandy was only slightly less than the danger inherent in a cross-dressing female scientist. At least the werewolf was an eligible bachelor.

Not that it was obvious, upon entering the shop, which one was the werewolf. To those with lesser noses, all the young gentlemen were cut from the same cloth – polite poodle-faking fops of the first order. Biffy worked hard to appear no more than one of them.

He did not look up as the strange werewolf entered his space. The shop was busy and he was at the very back, trying to convince a mother whose daughter had an aggressive nose that a small perch would detract from the protuberance rather than exaggerate. He was right, of course. Biffy was *always* right about hats.

However, the werewolf was *right there*. It wasn't polite to look away from his clients, although every fiber of his fuzzy self was urging him to raise his hackles and defend his territory. Not only because this was his hat shop, but because his hat shop was a front for the London Pack's safety dungeon. Biffy needed, with every part of his Alpha soul, to protect his pack's security.

The strange werewolf held back, waiting quietly on him. He heard the murmur of voices as one of his clavigers engaged the gentleman, attempting to steer him towards their shop next door – the one that purveyed men's headgear and accessories. The newcomer was polite, and so soft of voice that even Biffy's supernatural hearing could not determine what was said. But he clearly intended to stay, and to wait.

Simon let him be. Simon was not one to press himself upon a customer when unwanted. Or perhaps Simon was perceptive enough to see that the gentleman was interested in Biffy, not hats.

Biffy sniffed again. His nose told him nothing new. Foreign smells, yes, but this was someone's pack member, not a loner, which meant he was there as a representative or messenger in Biffy's territory, not as a challenger. He permitted himself a tiny sigh of relief.

He finished with the young lady and the perch, or, more properly, with the young lady's mother. She eventually came around to his gentle guidance, the trick being that the color of the hat was deemed a perfect complement to the girl's complexion, which was very fine indeed (nose notwithstanding). Biffy watched them walk to the counter to settle the account. He thought that the girl might do much better this season than she would have before the purchase of the hat. Hats were like that – necessary, even vital, to one's success on the marriage mart.

He spent a quiet moment rearranging the stock, ensuring the gap left by the perch would not be obvious. He collected his finer feelings, stamped civility and urbane sophistication over his werewolf instincts. *Someone in my territory!* He ensured his cuffs were peeking out perfectly from his jacket, and turned to meet the stranger.

The werewolf was standing behind a sea of hats. Madame Lefoux, the original owner, had chosen to dangle them all at the ends of long chains, so that they swayed softly at different lengths. A field through which shoppers could coo and drift. Biffy liked the design. It had a pleasing undersea quality, and so he kept it. The stranger stood on the other side of that field, peering through it at him.

He was a lean, undersized man, shrouded in a full cloak and a hat. Backlit by the gas wall sconces, it was difficult to see his face.

Biffy knew him instantly.

Yes, he smelled different. Yes, he had spoken too softly. But Biffy remembered that body and posture as if it were a childhood nursery rhyme – not word for word but the melody impressed upon his psyche in a way that would haunt him all his life.

Mine. My Beta.

He suddenly felt the tension he didn't even know he'd been holding. Tension since he'd assumed control of the pack several months earlier. Tension around need, and vacancy, and absence. He felt it now because it left him all at once. His knees wobbled. *Perhaps I've been holding it longer than two months. Perhaps I've been holding it twenty years.*

Professor Randolph Lyall had spent his very long life cultivating anonymity. He specialized in being impeccably easy to forget. He always dressed exactly under the height of fashion. His manners were perfectly quiet and perfectly polite, his customs designed to fade into the background. He was the ideal Beta, always there to observe and provide support, never to steal the limelight.

But Biffy *always* noticed Professor Lyall. Had done so from the very start. He'd noticed the set of Lyall's shoulders, and the curve of his neck, and the length of his eyelashes. Now, as Biffy moved towards Lyall, stalking, hunter-like, he noticed the way Lyall's sandy hair was longer, queued back in the military fashion. He watched the way he adjusted his waistcoat under Biffy's steady gaze. He remembered the way that waistcoat always contained precisely the right gadget for any occasion.

Biffy pushed the hats aside, careless of their movement. He was thinking too much about not running through them. He was concentrating too much on holding himself back. Heedless of watching claviger eyes and interested shoppers, Biffy closed the space between them.

Finally.

"You smell foreign," he accused Lyall, coming to a stop at last. Exactly the correct distance for a reunion among friends. Biffy was overcome, but he was never *that* overcome.

Professor Lyall smiled at him. It was a real smile too, one that crinkled the corners of his sand-colored eyes. "Good evening, Lord Falmouth."

"Professor." Biffy nodded his head in greeting. "Why did your smell change so much?"

"It's been a long time."

"You said it wouldn't feel so long to a werewolf."

"I lied."

"I know." Biffy held himself perfectly still. Afraid that if he moved, he would embarrass them both. They were, after all, in the middle of a hat shop. His mind blurred over with all the things he wanted to say, all the questions he wanted to ask, all the moments he wanted filled all at once. Thus all he could actually give his Beta were banalities.

"Welcome home."

Professor Lyall cocked his head, just slightly to the left, exactly as Biffy remembered. Did anyone else notice that he did that only when he was considering his words with extra care?

Biffy wanted to reach out and tuck a small bit of sandy hair behind Lyall's ear. Although, this being Lyall, not a hair was out of place. He wanted to ask stupid questions about why, and how, it was longer. He wanted to run his fingers over that jaw line, now covered by a well-tended and entirely modern bit of facial scruff. Darker than the hair on Lyall's head. Making him look even more foxlike. Biffy wanted to see if it was soft to the touch. He would need to glance around and see if they were under observation first. But he was afraid that if he looked away, Lyall would disappear in a puff of exotic-smelling smoke.

"It's good to be back."

"You've been in Egypt."

"The smell?"

"And the hair."

Lyall smiled. "You would comment on that. I see you've taken to keeping yours quite short on top."

As if Biffy had an option. "Was it nice being mortal again, if only for..." He allowed himself a touch at the length of those straight dirty-blond locks, silky smooth. "…two months?"

"I had to visit some old friends."

"I'm not complaining."

"No?"

"It took you long enough either way. Twenty years."

"So, what's two more months of waiting?" Lyall suggested an end to Biffy's reasoning, as if he had always known. As if he had not, in fact, been away at all.

Two more months was like two extra years. Like fumbling in the dark. Where were you? What took you so long? How could you leave me here to fend for myself?

Lyall was evaluating Biffy under his lashes, and then, with one of those impossibly subtle gestures full of incalculable meaning, he dropped his head back, lifting his chin to expose the length of his neck. Not so far as to be obvious, but almost. His voice went quieter and lower. "Alpha."

Biffy wanted to lick the line of his graceful throat.

So many things rolled up in that gesture: acknowledgment, power transfer, offering, acceptance. Much to his incalculable shame, lust spiked through Biffy. Possibly as a result of all four, possibly simply from his Beta's smell, for under Egypt, and India, and long sea journeys, Lyall still smelled of something else. Something familiar and half-remembered. Something yearned for and lost.

Mine.

The chin dipped, the sandy eyes lowered. Those

lashes spread out, long and pale against his cheeks. "So, are you ready?"

"Is anyone ready to be Alpha?"

"Only the ones doomed to fail think they are prepared."

"Are you ready to be back?"

"Of course. This is where I belong. And I already know how to be a Beta."

Biffy let out a breath. Happiness bubbled inside him like Lord Akeldama's stupid pink slurp, so unexpected it was all the more intoxicating. He slid into the wrong class for just a moment. "Bloody hell, Lyall, it took you long enough."

Professor Lyall barked out a surprised laugh. Then remembered himself.

Biffy wanted more than anything to reach for him, to pull him in close. But he was all nerves and worries. What had been pain and consolation twenty years earlier wasn't necessarily love now. Lyall had been there after Biffy changed, and held him, even knowing Biffy still loved Lord Akeldama. They had been *something* to each other. Necessity, perhaps. But that was two decades gone. Biffy wasn't a newly made, newly brokenhearted werewolf anymore.

And Lyall was his Beta. Biffy was pretty darn certain pack members weren't supposed to sleep with each other, let alone Alphas and Betas. That seemed a recipe for disaster. He'd certainly never heard nor read of such a relationship.

So, Biffy held himself apart and tried simply to be glad that his Beta was home. His Beta was there. It was, he thought, good enough. Or he would learn to let it be so.

CHAPTER THREE

A New Pack Member

He looks well enough. Lyall followed his Alpha's long, elegant strides out of the hat shop and into a hailed cab.

The silence in the hackney was awkward but not uncomfortable.

"How are they handling it?"

"Better than we hoped."

"And Channing?" The London Pack's strongest and most difficult member was their Gamma, Major Channing Channing of the Chesterfield Channings. Lyall had hated leaving Biffy to cope with him alone. But he could be coped with.

"He challenged."

"Of course he did." It was in a Gamma's nature to fight, to strike out, to react in anger to any change. It had its purpose within the pack. Providing, as much as a Beta did, its own kind of balance. But Channing was worse than most, more extreme.

"And I beat him back."

"Of course you did." Lyall was relieved to hear it but didn't let it show. He had worried. Biffy wasn't by nature a fighter. But he was Alpha, innately dominant, and blessed with Anubis Form. The ability to make new werewolves, which meant, regardless of his surface personality, no one should be able to challenge him for long. It's only that Biffy didn't come off as Alpha at first glance. Too delicate. Too pretty. Too civilized.

If we can find a way to meld these qualities, he will be everything we need henceforth.

Lyall's worry had been all for Channing, for Biffy's control. Channing was so much bigger, and so much angrier, he had thought there was a chance, just a chance...

"I'm glad you didn't have to kill him." He didn't like Channing, but he was, in his way, Lyall's brother if not friend.

"Me too." A wealth of feeling in those words from his Alpha. As if Biffy understood his worry, and the odd exasperated affection of centuries.

How horrible it would have been, not for Channing to die (although that was reasonably bad, for Channing) but for Biffy to have to cope with loss at his moment of Alpha acquisition. Not to mention a pack that had neither Beta nor Gamma.

"And how has he been since then?"

"Absent. He's now head of BUR and very much taken with the job. Did you know?"

Lyall inclined his head.

"Of course you knew." Biffy sat, still and poised across from him, the flickering lights of the lanterns making his too-pretty features shift in and out of focus.

Lyall knew those features well, had traced them with his fingertips. Straight nose with a tiny bit of up-tilt at the end, pointed chin just square enough to be masculine, lower lip slightly fuller than the upper one but together making a mouth almost feminine in its perfection.

"It is a good place for him, given that he no longer has his military position to distract him. He has worked for the War Office before. And the Home Office, I believe. He can handle the bureaucracy."

Biffy let out a slight breath.

Lyall could guess the source. "You came up with the idea to give him that job?"

Biffy nodded.

"Good instincts, Alpha."

He watched Biffy's shoulders relax slightly. "I had to fight for it. The Queen considers him a bit of a loose cannon, and it is by royal appointment. It could have gone horribly wrong."

"But it didn't. And a month in, he's doing well. Or so I hear."

Biffy's smile was more shaky than confident.

We will have to work on that.

It was late by the time they reached the new pack house. Biffy was proud of the place. It was much bigger than the previous town house. It had a large garden, and Blackheath was right there, beyond. Perhaps not big enough to be a full running ground, but big enough to give the whole place a feel of freedom and open fields, even in London.

Biffy was a city boy himself, always had been, but werewolves needed a sense of space, and this house gave it to them. He'd purchased it thinking that he needed to satisfy the shifting needs of his pack. They needed a greater sense of freedom than inner London allowed, but also, he wanted to give the populace a sense of their settling down.

The previous Alpha, Lord Maccon, had been very... well... much. As had his wife. *Very much* to tend to and *very much* to accommodate. Werewolves were pack – they liked to take care of their own. There had been the Maccon daughter as well, a handful herself, for all that she lived the bulk of her time with Lord Akeldama. Prior to Biffy's reign, the London Pack had withstood a time of upset and confusion. With Lord Maccon turning slowly mad under Alpha's curse, a stinky vampire living so close, politics and excitement all around them, it had been decades of aberration and unsettlement.

Biffy might be a new Alpha – different and young – but he knew it was his role to provide stability. And now with Lyall home, he felt that their legs, weak and newborn and shaky, could perhaps grow into something strong and sure.

Some instinct had urged him to buy a bigger house as a result. He wasn't certain if it was an Alpha's hope that they might be adding new members to their pack. Or some weird instinct that suggested, now that the London Pack Alpha was a civilized gentleman with a marked preference for other gentlemen, some of his pack might consider marriage their duty.

They had abstained for decades. Lady Maccon was a lot to look after, and not the type of female to brook other ladies in her domain. However, werewolves were allowed to marry under British law. Even encouraged to do so, where widows with children were concerned. Werewolves, being undead, could not (of course) have children of their own. But the pack structure was considered an excellent welfare resource for a worthy gentlewoman who was too long a spinster or too old a widow. Such marriages were thought good for the pack, bringing (as society deemed it) the taming forces of womanhood to an otherwise worryingly masculine environment.

Biffy had a feeling, now that things had shaken out for his own pack, that his wolves might start courting. Their new Alpha would bring no new wife of his own – he was not inclined. It seemed likely that some of them might hunt wives for themselves. This both thrilled and worried Biffy. But made it absolutely necessary to invest in a very large house.

Not that I'd mind women or even children around the place. I miss Alexia. Of course, Biffy missed Lord Maccon for the responsibility that had not been Biffy's while the man still ruled. But he missed Lady Maccon for the sheer joy of a woman's company. He might prefer men in his bed, but one could have too much of a good thing in one's life. And his pack was very masculine, sometimes overwhelmingly so.

Such thoughts kept him mostly silent throughout the drive home.

"There it is," he said, pointing out the house to Lyall, a little anxious, hoping his Beta approved of the place.

It was almost a mansion, set apart and practically within the heath. This gave it excellent, and defensible, positioning and a good aspect. Biffy had purchased it off the crown and at a reduced rate, partly because, the queen claimed, while Falmouth title came with lands in Cornwall, it did not come with a house in town, and he did need something appropriate to his position.

It was a well-balanced Georgian building,

whitewashed stone with a low roof. No columns or Greek stylings, it had many small windows with charming lemon-colored shutters (Biffy took no chances with sunlight) and a few larger bay windows with arches on the first level. It was pleasant, the type of house built for solid country gentry with nothing to prove – unpretentious, but warm and welcoming.

Biffy was tradesman enough (after decades in the hat business) not to protest a good deal when it was thrust upon him.

Most of the pack was likely out. It was a few hours until morning, and they would be about their various places of business, checking in with the regiments or guards, attending social matters at their club, or otherwise occupied. The moon being nearer new than full, Biffy wasn't concerned. He hoped that the squabbling had been left over the breakfast table and that the house was now peaceful.

He was looking forward to a nice cup of tea and good gossip with his Beta before a warm fire.

He led Lyall through the wrought-iron gate in the garden's stone wall, and up the path to the front door somewhat proudly. Lyall perked up, seeming less tired as he took in his new home with bright hazel eyes.

"Welcome to Falmouth House, Professor Lyall." Biffy pushed open the big door to find... total and utter chaos.

Lyall was gobsmacked. There was no politer way of putting it. And not by their new residence, although it was bigger than Woolsey Castle, much more welcoming, and impeccably decorated. He expected no less from his new Alpha.

No, he had never before heard his pack in such a confused state. The multitude of voices, all familiar and all at once, mixed in with the screams of some creature apparently in the throes of slow dismemberment.

"Well." Biffy was clearly mortified. "This is embarrassing. I did so want to impress you."

"The house is lovely, Alpha. But perhaps we should ascertain the nature of the disturbance?" Lyall put down his small traveling case in the grand entranceway and followed the noise into what appeared to be the drawing room, and the eye of the storm.

Biffy trailed behind him.

Of the pack, Adelphus, Quinn, Phelan, Hemming, Rafe, Ulric, and Zev were all home. Channing was likely still at work. Riehard was also missing. *Probably on assignment. I'll have to get his thoughts on the past few months as soon as he returns.* Riehard was a kindred spirit, very observant, preferring the background to center stage, and mostly even-tempered.

Lyall took in his seven pack mates, assorted clavigers, and household staff in one quick sweep. Biffy came in after and stood staring with his mouth open.

The pack was flapping about in a discombobulated manner like a flock of starving pigeons that had just been thrown a scattering of highly desirable bread scraps. Since most of them were on the larger end of the masculine spectrum, this was a lot of flapping for even the impressive drawing room to contain.

Hemming stood at the center of the cyclone and seemed to be emitting a very high-pitched, extremely loud wailing sound.

Ah, not Hemming but something Hemming is holding. Is that...

"Hemming," Biffy barked from slightly too close to Lyall. Lyall shivered. "Is that *an infant* you have clutched to your breast?"

"Hot water," Adelphus was insisting. "Don't human offspring always need hot water? Should I ask Cook to put the kettle to boil? He's making a great deal of noise. Perhaps two kettles?"

"And clean linens? Or bandages, do we need bandages?" That was Quinn, his quizzical brow even more quizzical than usual, his dark hair spiked up as if he'd been running his hands through it.

"Oh, for goodness' sake, Hemming isn't in the act of giving birth! We need milk. Or is he old enough for mushy food? What do you think?" *Phelan at his most aristocratic.* His deep voice rumbled through the chaos.

"Are there teeth? Isn't age determined by the presence or absence of teeth?" Rafe this time, bouncing about, looking scruffy and worried.

"I think that's in horses, not humans," corrected Phelan.

"I think mushy food. Peas or potatoes or porridge or something?" Quinn again.

"Do all mushy foods start with *p* according to you?" wondered Ulric mildly from one side of the room.

"Why is he crying so much? Hemming, rock him back and forth." Rafe looked over Hemming's shoulder.

"No, no, don't do that. Swaddle him and hold him tightly. He needs reassurance, poor little mite. Abandoned like that." Zev, dark eyes wide with fear.

"Should I sing?" Hemming this time. "Aren't you supposed to sing to nippers?"

"No!" several voices at once. Werewolves gained many things upon achieving immortality, but a sense of pitch wasn't one of them.

Ulric stayed in the background, looking concerned but not involved. He could get that way in a crisis, withdrawn and reserved, but this was even more than customary. Lyall paused, examining his countenance for hidden meaning. *Is he pulling away from the pack?*

Ulric registered his presence, and a wide smile slashed across his impossibly handsome face.

Lyall tilted his head at his old friend.

Through all the chatter, the clavigers rushed about, gathering great piles of throws and blankets, putting them on and then off the bundle in Hemming's arms. Occasionally, by accident or design, one would fall over Hemming's head. Staff dashed off, following some causally thrown-out order, then came running back in with whatever had been requested. The tables were now piled with linen bandages, bowls of porridge, pitchers of hot water, a basket of dried flowers, assorted bottles of medicinals, a pair of large woolly slippers, and, for some unaccountable reason, a set of curling tongs. *Who in my pack uses curling tongs?* Biffy imagined it was Channing and amused himself greatly.

The werewolves circled about Hemming and his bundle. Fingers were shoved at the bundle. Food was shoved at the bundle. The bundle wiggled and screamed ever louder.

"I have never heard anything yell so much," said Ulric, wandering over to them. "Not even Lord Maccon. How can such a tiny thing make so much noise?"

Lyall looked at Biffy, measured. *What will you do, Alpha?*

Biffy narrowed his eyes at Lyall for one second and then cut through the hubbub to where Hemming stood.

He was no imposing presence, although the man had near-perfect posture, and a near perfect posterior, which was imposing enough as far as Lyall was concerned. But his movements were so beautiful and his appearance so impeccable, he managed to be intimidating for all he was the smallest in the room. *Apart from me, of course.*

Hemming was entirely the opposite of his Alpha, a large, bumbling, salt-of-the-earth breed of chap. Big, blond, and rangy but with almost delicate features. The others referred to him, when Hemming wasn't listening, as *sensitive*. He had wistful, watery blue eyes – which were currently wide and panicked – and subtle but thick sideburns. He was the kind of man to be depicted in art as mucking out stalls and pitching hay. He likely had been, since he'd once modeled for various well-known painters who specialized in rural depictions of manor houses and handsome farmers and ducks and the like. *I wonder if he still does.* Saddled with a baby, he looked utterly overwhelmed. Although Lyall knew exactly how it had landed in his arms. Hemming was widely thought of by the entire pack as the gentlest among them.

"Oh, heaven forfend! What do I do? Why won't he stop crying?" Hemming tried bouncing the tiny thing. The screaming persisted.

Biffy marched up to him.

Hemming's desperate gaze landed on his Alpha and, to Lyall's delight, instantly turned to one of profound relief. "Oh, thank the fates. Here."

The squalling bundle was thrust into Biffy's arms.

It wasn't that Lyall didn't *like* children. It's simply that they were, by and large, quite messy. Lyall abhorred a mess. This one proved to live up to his assessment.

Biffy took the little creature and cradled it up against his shoulder, and began patting its back. This action caused the child to stop screaming.

It seems my new Alpha has untold depths. Or perhaps it's only that as the youngest werewolf amongst us, he has more recent experience with the procreative habits of mortals.

Then the infant emitted an entirely ungentlemanly burp and spilled what appeared to be most of its dinner down the back of Biffy's beautiful burgundy gabardine evening jacket.

The Alpha's face! Lyall swallowed his smile with difficulty.

Biffy jerked the offensive creature away from said jacket. The baby instantly began screaming again, perhaps not quite so loudly. Biffy thrust it back into Hemming's arms.

"Oh, my goodness, Alpha, I am so sorry! I know how you feel about your jackets. James! Quickly!" Adelphus, properly horrified, waved frantically at one of the clavigers.

"My lord!" A good-looking young blunt rushed Biffy. "Let me take that for you."

This is, no doubt, James. Lyall assessed the lad. All the clavigers would be new to him. There were only a few home at the moment, wringing their hands and trying to be useful. Unless the traditions of pack had drastically altered, which Lyall doubted, most of the clavigers were off duty at this time of night. *Thank goodness for small mercies. As half of them are usually actors, their presence would only have added to the general drama of a baby among the werewolves.*

Lyall watched as James attempted to help Biffy remove his coat. *Impressive that he still manages to wear them so tight.* This unfortunately revealed the fact that some of the regurgitated fluids also decorated Biffy's silver cravat, brocade burgundy and silver waistcoat, and white shirt as well.

See what I mean? Babies, messy.

Clearly desperate to be useful, James then began stripping Biffy of every piece of clothing.

Lyall was not at all averse to this turn of events.

Meanwhile, the chaos around them continued. Exacerbated, perhaps, by the Alpha being covered in spit-up. Now all the werewolves were worried for the safety of their new charge. Alphas had tempers.

Lyall stayed quiet and calm, waiting to see if Beta interference would be necessary. He was trying to get a read on the currents of his new-yet-old pack. Some things most certainly would have changed over the last twenty years.

And some things definitely had not.

"I'm sure he didn't mean it!" That would be Rafe, of course. Rafe looked like a bruiser but was in fact a big-hearted softy, prone to accommodating strays. Their previous house had come with a family of alley cats adjacent, who'd discovered early on that Rafe was one for *accidentally* leaving the hunt's rabbit liver out for them rather than eating it himself.

Rafe was currently trying to pet the baby's head. No doubt wondering if the child liked liver. And if he should go hunt him something fresh.

Lyall sensed his Alpha's frustration rise.

Biffy batted off his claviger. "Do stop attempting to get me naked, James. I know you've been trying for months, but now is not the time."

Lyall certainly hoped *that* was a joke.

"But sir, the stains will set!"

"And so I can buy new garments. At the moment, the state of my dress seems the least of our problems. Take the coat away and tend to it, do."

Lyall was only a little sad to see the lad leave – Biffy was still in his shirt, after all.

Biffy, with an exasperated sigh, took the child back.

The infant quieted, perhaps simply because Biffy was not harrowed by his presence. Children could sense distress, he always thought. Biffy hoisted the little chap to his shoulder, patting him again. Hoping there would be no additional dietary return engagements, but not really minding now that he was only wearing a shirt.

It is a marker of my acceptance of my own werewolf state that I am not self-conscious about wearing so little in front of so many in my own drawing room.

The baby stopped screaming and the pack settled into awed relief – the quiet after the storm.

"Alpha, how'd you do that?"

Biffy sighed. "I've eleven siblings. Or I did, you know, *before*. Only three of them were older than me. I've more than enough experience with babies. Now, Adelphus, this boy here is very young. We will need a wet nurse. You and Quinn go inquire at the church – the local pastor might know of some able-bodied local lady."

He continued issuing orders, feeling rather proudly in charge. It was nice, for a change, to know more about something than the rest of his pack. Most of them were at least sixty years older than he, many of them three or four times that; it was a rare privilege to be commanding by reason of capability, not simply Alpha nature. *This must be how Lyall feels.*

"Hemming, where did the child originate?" Biffy directed his stare at the original holder of the goods.

"He was left on our doorstep, Alpha. Simply, you know, there. Wriggling."

Biffy called Adelphus and Quinn back before they could leave. "Also see if the pastor has any idea who the infant's mother might be. Go by the workhouse as well. I take it there is one nearby?"

"Yes, Alpha," said Adelphus smartly.

"I know where it is, Alpha," said Rafe.

"Good, then Rafe, you go to the workhouse while Quinn and Adelphus go to the church. If they're asleep at the rectory, rouse them. They know we're in the neighborhood and should be expecting the occasional nighttime call. I went by and had tea after we first arrived." Biffy made a face. "That said, I advise against drinking the tea, if he offers. It's perishingly weak."

"Yes, Alpha!" The three turned to leave. The clavigers scattered ahead of them in search of hats and coats.

Only then did they catch sight of Lyall, standing in his diffident way, slightly to the back of the room.

Lyall's eyes crinkled in a suppressed smile as the (there was no better way of putting it) ecstatic squeals of the first three caused the rest of the puck to swivel around and stare at him.

Quinn, Adelphus, and Rafe descended upon him.

"Professor! You're home!" That was Quinn.

"Randolph, how delightful. It's been too long. Far too

long!" Adelphus looked genuinely pleased, a rarity from he who liked to pretend ennui at the state of the universe.

Rafe pounced upon their returned pack mate and gave him a hug. Rafe was like that.

Hemming instantly followed.

For the moment, Biffy was left in sole possession of the child. His own heart warmed at his pack's evident delight. Their Beta was back. *My Beta is back. They are so free and happy with him.*

Lyall looked quietly pleased by the attention. "Well, gentlemen, while I am happy to be home and delighted to see you all again, did your Alpha not just issue direct orders?" A gentle rebuke.

The drawing room was instantly less crowded as Adelphus, Quinn, and Rafe slapped top hats to their heads, twirled great coats about their massive shoulders, and dashed out into the cold December night.

Biffy nodded to his Beta, pleased to be acknowledged so directly. Then he resumed issuing orders, aware now that, with Lyall's silent observation, the rest of the pack would obey instantly. He was unsure if he was happy with this swift change in attitude. It would be a sad kind of Alpha that required his Beta to chivvy his pack into the simplest tasks.

Biffy sent staff off about the house to retrieve warm milk (not ideal but better than nothing for now) and Zev to find a hatbox of appropriate size and shape to make up a temporary bassinet. They had a surfeit of hatboxes, given Biffy's occupation.

The baby began to settle, thank heavens.

Biffy felt it safe to sit down as the little boy fell asleep, profoundly exhausted by his emotional display, no doubt.

Well, he should be – imagine making such a fuss amongst strangers.

Hemming came to sit next to him. "He's much cuter when he's not screaming."

"They usually are."

Phelan came around the back of the settee to look down as well. He loomed rather too much but couldn't help it, poor fellow. Bit of a loomer, was Phelan. "What shall we call him? I mean, presumably he belongs to somebody and I'm sure they gave him some kind of name, but we should have a moniker in the interim."

"Why? Won't *baby* do?" Ulric seemed to deem it safe to come away from the corner he'd been keeping warm and the hat stand he'd been keeping company. He held himself, however, about as stiffly as the hat stand, as though the sleeping infant might suddenly lurch in his direction.

"How about Ulric the Second?" suggested Hemming, with a grin.

Zev had returned with a good-sized hat box and now had an arm around Lyall and was whispering something into the Beta's ear. Biffy wasn't sure how he felt about that kind of intimacy.

It seemed to be nothing significant to Lyall, as the Beta merely ruffled his friend's hair and said, "I'm sure it's fine. Stop worrying."

Zev ducked his head. "I'm glad you're home, Professor."

"I'm glad to be home." Lyall came over, stood a little apart from them all, and crinkled his eyes at them affectionately. "How about Robin? It being, you know, that time of year?"

"Robin?" said Biffy, stupidly.

"Like the bird."

"I like it!" Hemming grinned. "What do you think, Robin?"

The baby cooed.

"There, see, he likes it, too."

"There goes my legacy," said Ulric, smiling for a change.

"Now, what do we do with Robin next?" Zev seemed worried. He liked plans. Biffy gave a little wince – poor Zev. It was hard to keep to any kind of plan with a baby around.

"Sing at it? One of the clavigers could sing? James has a rather fine tenor," suggested Phelan. Biffy wondered, not for the first time, if Phelan missed his own talent in that arena. Well before Biffy was born, Phelan had been one of England's most renowned basso profundos. Fortunately, giving it all up for immortality did not seem to have left him bitter, only arrogant.

Lyall glided closer to join them all clustered about the sleeping infant. "I think he's fine where he is."

His hazel eyes – still slightly crinkled in pleasure – were not on the child.

Biffy was not entirely sure a Beta should look with eyes like that at his Alpha. But he couldn't deny how much he enjoyed the affectionate regard.

He lifted the little one up and nested him more securely in the crook of his arm.

CHAPTER FOUR

The Blessings of Fatherhood

Lyall could never have anticipated how blisteringly attractive he found a man coming over competent with a baby. Especially considering that he, Professor Lyall, while undoubtedly pack-minded, had never impressed anyone by being family-minded.

It was rather inconvenient, this surge of unwanted attraction, since he had concluded that Biffy had no interest in pursuing their previous dalliance. After all, the man hadn't even touched him since he returned. He barely even looked at him.

Lyall was not stupid. He was perfectly capable of understanding unspoken messages. He was resolved to think no further on his Alpha in *that* way. It shouldn't be all that difficult – what they'd had together was a mere comforting of bodies for a short time, many years ago (putting aside, of course, how hot it burned and how well they suited). But it turned out a man in only a thin white shirt with a baby to his chest might be a previously undiscovered lust object.

Odd, given I'm not particularly fond of babies, and

old enough to have learned every one of my carnal preferences by now.

Lyall shook his head at himself and resolved to push the image out of his mind.

He retreated upstairs and began busily unpacking. He hadn't much with him, only his trusty carpet bag with a few necessities. The bag was constructed of good Brussels carpeting and unquestionable workmanship. The vendor had claimed, when he bought it, it would last a lifetime. Human lifetime, one assumed, not werewolf. Ninety years and still going strong, and Professor Lyall had learned how to pack everything he needed in that bag and on his person. Of course, he had trunks with him from India and Egypt. If nothing else, he'd stocked up on gifts of fine fabrics, fabulous spices, and the occasional weapon or gadget for the truly discerning. He'd leave instructions with one of the clavigers for someone to visit the old pack house, come daylight, and retrieve them.

Zev offered him a rather undersized room. "I know it's small, but it has the best view." His old friend and pack mate wasn't really concerned about the space – he knew Lyall's tastes well. "Although, of course, any of us would switch, if you require it." Unspoken was the acknowledgment of Lyall's rank.

But Lyall was happy with the room. He didn't need much space, being small himself (for a werewolf), and he preferred a pleasing view. This one looked out on Blackheath, and he could almost smell the mist rising in the morning air. Not that he saw mornings often. Daylight was never healthy for a werewolf, even when one was old enough and strong enough to withstand it. Still, he liked knowing it would happen and he could see it if he dared.

Unsaid was the fact that the room was adjacent to Biffy's master suite. Lyall supposed the others either remembered previous intimacies, and this was tacit approval to resume them – *sadly, no chance of a resurgence.* Or it was simply the pack indicating that the Beta should be nearest the Alpha. Which wasn't wrong.

I wonder if Biffy still has nightmares.

Feeling modestly settled, Lyall headed back downstairs. They still had an hour before dawn. *Long winter nights.* There he found that Adelphus and Quinn had returned.

The church had proved unhelpful.

"Apparently, the pastor has been having issues with a newly arrived Episcopal counter-service, whose members are noted for being rather unfriendly. His attention has been distracted from his flock as a result." Quinn looked concerned by this as he reported it.

Adelphus added, "He tenders his profound apologies."

Biffy looked up, eyes narrowed. "And something more?"

Good. He's in tune with their mannerisms.

Adelphus looked pained. "*And* he suggests we attend one of his midnight services."

Biffy nodded. "It's not a bad idea. We should integrate better into the community if we did. Your thoughts, Professor?"

Such easy command. And still he doubts himself.

Lyall said, "Perhaps not as a full pack. We are rather large in both individual size and numbers. We have been known to overwhelm laymen en masse."

"Small groups, you think? Or even just pairs?" Biffy considered. "Yes, and spread out the visits over the next few months. Professor, can you draw up a schedule? Leave off Channing, of course. He's too much. And Riehard is out of town until Thursday week." He glared around at the pack. "But the others can go. You'll wear your Sunday best or I'll know the reason why."

No doubt every one of them now boasts pristine Sunday best. Lyall was not yet certain in the manner and style of his new Alpha's rule, but he could be confident in Biffy's militant insistence on appropriate attire. Lord Maccon hadn't cared how his werewolves dressed, Lord Falmouth absolutely *did.* The London pack would be the best-dressed werewolves in all the Empire or their Alpha would birth kittens. (Which, given his gender and species, was a manifold impossibility.)

"Also, it's an opportunity to gather local gossip," Lyall suggested delicately.

Biffy looked back at the baby, which was now asleep in his lap, in a dead fish kind of way. "Of course. See if we can catch wind of Robin's relations. Unfortunate that the pastor couldn't help us with that."

Lyall added, "A rival church is also concerning." Outside of the Anglican faith, very few religions embraced the supernatural. To have a pack and a, perhaps, anti-immortal church occupying Greenwich at the same time could cause civil unrest.

"All the more reason to integrate ourselves into the community and ingratiate ourselves with the establishment." Biffy glared about, but the pack mainly seemed resigned to the occasional night of worship for the sake of Greenwich peace and harmony.

The Christmas season is soon upon us. Lyall pondered. "I shall send round a brace of pheasant to the pastor next time we hunt as well."

Rafe returned at that juncture, fortunately, having met with greater success at the workhouse. He was trailing a buxom young lady who was all smiles. He introduced her as a Mrs Whybrew and their prospective wet nurse. She had a baby tucked under one arm, which appeared to be her issue, if appearances were anything to go by. The baby boasted the same cornflower eyes, wide face, and honey hair. Mrs Whybrew was rather too rough in her language and rather too forward in her manner and address for Lyall's taste, but he had to admit that would serve her well, dealing with werewolves.

He noticed that Biffy winced a bit. But Biffy was even more a snob than he. One of his more adorable qualities.

I should certainly not be thinking of my Alpha as adorable.

Mrs Silence Whybrew was a widow, her husband's overenthusiastic celebration of their own blessed event having occasioned a drunken tumble over an ill-placed whitebait stall directly in front of the local music hall. The resulting pinwheeling collapse was thought to be a modern interpretive dance-commentary on the current state of dockside fish-trading facilities. He was thus left to expire and did so, with no one the wiser until he began to smell worse than the whitebait.

Mrs Whybrew delivered this tragic tale with an unprecedented degree of amusement. "Oh, you're welcome to laugh, boyos."

Rafe and Hemming were both struggling to respect the gravity of her loss (as opposed to the ridiculousness of its execution). Lyall felt his own lips twitch, and he was usually the best of them.

"He was a right ol' sod. I'm no' ashamed to say I was plumb glad to be rid of 'im, 'cepting for that it landed me in the workhouse. 'Course now I'm 'ere, and this seems a fine place to be."

She grinned around at the assembled large gentlemen. "And grateful for the attention, I don't mind saying."

Lyall wished she wouldn't. Silence Whybrew seemed a startlingly ill-named individual.

She continued to defy her moniker. "You're a fine lot of muffins, aren't you?"

Zev blushed. Hemming's mouth dropped open. Rafe started to snicker.

She strode forward towards Biffy. "So lemme see to the little 'un."

Lyall slid like oil in front of her. No one, but *no one,* approached his Alpha without being properly vetted first.

"Oh, well, then. Who're you?"

"Mrs Whybrew? Perhaps if you'd take a seat over there, I will bring the child to you."

"Well then, if you insist, m' boy. Funny ol' things, you werewolves, aren't you, then?"

Lyall scooped the baby off Biffy's lap (Biffy giving him an inscrutable look) and deposited it on Mrs Whybrew's. Robin did not amend his floppy state, and she seemed remarkably capable of handling two at once.

She looked down on the infant with genuine interest and affection.

At least there is no artifice to this woman.

"Aw now, ain't he sweet? We'll do nicely, he and I and little Gracie here." She grinned around at the assembled pack. "I've more milk than my Gracie-girl can handle." Her eyes shone with hope. "If you'd like me here, I could get up with him in the night and all sorts."

Everyone looked at Biffy.

Mrs Whybrew finally realized her breach of protocol.

"Oh, 'eck, you're the new Alpha, ain't you? Didn't know your lot came so pretty. I thought you was one of them clavigers. I didn't mean anything by..."

She trailed off, blushing crimson at her many gaffes.

"My mama always said I couldna stop my mouth with anything short of a dirigible, it was tha' big."

Biffy quirked an eyebrow at her.

"I beg pardon, m'lord. But I'm a good woman, I surely am. I'd do my best for you." She straightened, but her care for the two infants in her lap didn't waver. "Thinking I ought stop talking now."

"Why alter a habit you've clearly no intent to change?" Biffy spoke at last, seeming genuinely curious rather than cruel.

Mrs Whybrew laughed. "Oh, aye! You and me, we're fine, aren't we, m'lord?"

Biffy grinned at that, his sweet, solemn face suddenly suffused with aching beauty. It'd been a very long time since Lyall had seen him smile like that.

"Welcome to the pack, Mrs Whybrew."

Lyall sighed. That was his cue.

"Perhaps Mrs Whybrew and I might step into the conservatory for a little chat. Alpha, if you're certain?"

Biffy nodded.

A short interview later, Lyall concluded that Mrs Whybrew was a salt-of-the-earth type with no immediately apparent character flaws – aside from a certain breeziness of manner. Older than she appeared, crass and unashamed, but nothing seriously debilitating. She was utterly without malice or guile. While Lyall wasn't certain how well she would fit in with the pack in the long term, she seemed entirely well suited as a temporary salve to the unexpected fatherhood that had been thrust upon them. Or thrust upon their doorstep.

They agreed upon terms so generous, the lady in question began to cry in gratitude. Lyall gave her a handkerchief and saw her installed, plus measly belongings, in the nursery. The babies remained gratifyingly uninterested in the proceedings and settled down under Mrs Whybrew's practiced touch with no further histrionics.

Then, because he could, Lyall sent Zev off in pursuit of some decent clean clothes for all three of their new additions – Gracie, Robin, and Mrs Whybrew. He included an extensive list of other necessities that Mrs Whybrew claimed were not urgent but would certainly smooth matters over with the infants in question. Things like blankets, and knitwear, cloth for nappies, and associated cleaning apparatus of such elaborate and complex nature that Lyall really would prefer not to think about their use.

By dawn, everything was settled and the pack was asleep.

Channing returned directly before sunup and gave Lyall a grumpy look out of ice-blue eyes.

"You back, then?"

"Yes, Channing, I'm back."

"Good. It's been hell without you. And if you tell anyone I said that, I'll categorically deny it."

"Good to know where I stand."

"Nothing's changed there."

"Just so you're aware, there are two babies and a wet nurse now in residence."

That managed to ruffle Channing's arrogant icy air. "Not... yours?"

"How would that even be possible?"

"I wouldn't put it past you."

Lyall decided to take that as a weird kind of compliment. "No, Channing, one was left as a deposit, and then the other two followed as compound interest."

"I find that's all too often the case with women and children."

"Channing, I don't know why, but I believed that twenty years would improve your personality."

"God's teeth, man, I don't know why you believed that either. I'm going to bed – keep the brats away from me."

Lyall rolled his eyes and took to his own bed as well. It was a nice bed in a sweet room. His own beloved, if eccentric, pack was once more around him, and his Alpha was one door over. *My Alpha.* He found himself smiling in a manner he was certain must appear foolish. Fortunately, there was absolutely no one to see.

The smile turned wicked (in a manner Lyall would never allow outside the privacy of his own bedroom). There was something thrilling in the prospect of knowing Channing would have to cope with screaming babies. Thrilling in a different way came the memory of that small body curled against Biffy's chest. There was also a certain warmth and knowledge that between them, he and his Alpha, had managed to cope elegantly with a crisis, small and wiggly though it may be.

What a homecoming.

With any luck, thought Lyall as he drifted off, *Robin's rightful parents will have been found by the time the sun sets and the pack is up and about once more.*

Of course, that didn't happen. In fact, it got worse. Because when the werewolves came down to breakfast the next evening, it was to find that yet another child had been left on their doorstep.

If Robin gave Mrs Whybrew and the clavigers any trouble during the daylight hours, no one reported it. The werewolves slept snug in their beds undisturbed.

Biffy awoke feeling more rested than he had since first assuming Alpha. This could, no doubt, be attributed to Lyall's presence in the room adjoining. To have his Beta home – so capable and so calm. He had handled all of last night's excitement with good-humored efficiency. *I am a lucky Alpha.*

Contemplating Lyall's curled and sleeping form, so close, warm and soft and smelling of spices and foreign lands, was less restful. The sleep fled Biffy's brain, and in its place came yearning. To crawl in next to that warmth. To rub against the softness of his skin, to rub away those foreign smells. To mark him and claim him, for pack, of course, but also as lover. *To make him not just my Beta. But mine.*

Probably not a good thought to start the night with.

Biffy rang for his claviger to help him dress.

James took slightly longer than usual to arrive and was in a decided tizzy.

"Out with it, dear boy, you're practically vibrating."

"We've had another one, my lord!" James buttoned up Biffy's shirt-front with nimble fingers.

"Another what, James?"

"Sorry, sir. Another baby on the doorstep."

"You're having me on."

"No, sir, it'd be in very poor taste if I were, and I should try to be more original about it."

"Well, that's something. No, not the blue waistcoat, not with a brown suit. Are you mad?"

"Your pardon, sir. Not thinking right, sir."

"I should say not." Biffy cut no slack on the matter of waistcoats. Or better said, all slack was already cut, because his waistcoats fit perfectly and were never subject to debate or jocularity.

James selected a gold paisley instead, which wasn't exactly what Biffy would have chosen but was good enough and he didn't want to upset the boy further.

"A girl child this time, sir. Mrs Whybrew says this one's older, on solid food but not yet of an age to speak much by way of information. Although she seems to have the capacity for *mummy* and *daddy* – Mrs Whybrew and the coat rack are receiving *mummy*, and the pack, clavigers, and that mermaid sculpture behind the card table are under the auspices of *daddy*."

Biffy shuddered delicately. "Not the mermaid Ulric insists reminds him of his misspent youth?"

James's eyes twinkled. "The very one, sir."

Biffy regularly threatened to accidentally stumble into that mermaid. It was quite hideous, being of that porcelain variety favored by grandmothers, with too many shelves to fill. Her tail faded to insipid blue and her skin was rather wan and splotchy. The mermaid herself wore an expression of profound discomfort, and everyone (except Ulric) was under the impression she ought to be put out of her misery.

Biffy sighed. *It's not that I mind living in a household full of strapping men, but I could wish werewolfism conferred alongside more aesthetic understanding and less wet-fur smell.* "So, the hunt for the parents of these infants is once more on? Is it possible the new one is related to Robin?"

"Mrs Whybrew says she thinks not. The ages are too close to permit such." James looked pained, as if the very idea of the calculations behind this assessment troubled him.

"Very well. I'd best go down. Just a simple knot tonight, James. With all this fuss around the house, I very much doubt I'll be going out on the town this evening."

James looked relieved. He was new to Biffy and not, thus far, a standout. He'd been given various complicated knots to study but hadn't yet mastered any. Biffy had given serious consideration to the hiring of a proper valet, but werewolves were supposed to employ clavigers as personal gentlemen, and James was *trying*. Unfortunately, it meant Biffy's cravat, more often than not, looked as if it were *trying* too. He'd had to re-tie his at the club more than once.

Biffy wondered if there was a school for valets he could send James off to for a brush-up. He was a good, even-tempered lad, for all he trod the boards, but his knot work... quite, quite lacking.

Biffy slid into his coat. James gave a critical eye to his lapels.

I suppose I can't be too harsh on the chap. He is almost as new to being a claviger as I am to being an Alpha.

Biffy patted James on the shoulder. "Good lad, thank you."

James blushed and dipped his head.

Easy as that, is it? Poor fellow, have I been a horrible grump these past few months?

"You can head off about your business. You have a performance tonight, I believe?"

"Yes, my lord."

"Carry on."

"Thank you, sir." And James was off.

Biffy followed him with a little more dignity. He paused in the hallway outside Lyall's door. Then, because he wished to stop second-guessing himself, knocked sharply.

Lyall opened the door himself.

"Alpha?" He appeared to be in mid-toilette and was knotting his own cravat, if the loose material around his neck and the absence of a claviger were anything to go by.

"Ah, good, professor. A moment of your time?"

"Of course, Alpha, if you don't mind me..." He waved at his neck.

"I could call a claviger for you. I'm sure there is one to spare."

"No, no, I prefer to see to myself."

Biffy smiled. Of course he did. "Well, perhaps I might help?"

Lyall blushed at the offer. It wasn't proper, of course, but everyone knew Biffy was particular about neckwear.

"I'd be honored," said Lyall, because they both knew it was all he could say.

Biffy stepped in and moved towards him.

This might have been a miscalculation. It brought them too close together. Biffy's fingers, ordinarily so nimble about a cravat, came over fat and fumbling. Lyall's scent was still peppered with spices and healed sand, although there was starting to be more of the memory of him there, underneath. The scent of the real Lyall. Lost lovers. Old Betas. Salt and sweet and caring.

Biffy breathed a little less deeply, because he

desperately wanted to do the opposite.

Lyall, for his part, remained perfectly motionless under his Alpha's touch.

Biffy coiled the length of cloth about Lyall's neck, twice – a deft twist here, a fold there, ending with one clean simple stab of a very plain cravat pin. He stayed close one more moment, fiddling a little longer with the shape of the knot and tucking the fall. Because he wasn't ready to stop.

Lyall's very stillness was a memory itself, of a nested presence that had once held him still, too, for a time. Held him together and whole, when the world was shattering around them both.

He stepped back, too much all at once. *I cannot abuse my power as his Alpha. We cannot be what we were.* Lyall had given him no indication that a renewal of advances would be welcome. Their communication over the years had been sporadic and polite. He had not the courage to try and no incentive to hope. Another part of his past that he must let go.

"It seems we have another stray?"

Lyall let out a tiny, shaky breath.

Oh, no, thought Biffy, *he is not indifferent. Now what do I do?*

He thought to step back in towards the slighter man. Just one more touch. His cheek, perhaps?

But Lyall turned away in pursuit of his jacket.

His waistcoat was so plain it was almost an insult to his station, although not quite. His jacket was only slightly more appropriate. But Biffy knew it was Lyall's way, to stay in the background, to make no fuss with manners, or opinions, or dress. Always oddly attractive, that cultivated invisibility. As if Biffy were the only one capable of really noticing Lyall. Because Biffy had always been aware of him, whenever Lyall was near. Which was why he was there now, alone with his Beta. Too alone for his own needs to permit, really.

I must be careful in future. I fear I over-stress the Beta-Alpha relationship. I make it mean too much. Because I want it to mean more than it does.

"Another baby was left on the doorstep?" Lyall guessed.

Of course, Lyall would apprehend the truth without need for an explanation. Nevertheless, Biffy relayed what James had said.

"Well, at least we have Mrs Whybrew."

"Small mercies."

"This can't be allowed to continue."

"No, I agree."

"Your plan, Alpha?"

"I was thinking of pulling everyone I could in for the evening and setting us all to a concerted effort at tracking down any parents. Perhaps you might consider taking wolf form and putting that most excellent nose of yours to good use?"

"You want me to do some tracking?"

"If you aren't averse."

"No, Alpha, I think that is an excellent idea. Perhaps first I should talk with the clavigers, reintroduce myself, before they depart for the evening? That way, I can set a plan for further investigation during daylight hours tomorrow, in case we cannot solve this before morning."

This is why Lyall is such a good Beta. Always prepared to offer support but also suggestions.

Biffy allowed himself a full, warm smile of gratitude. "Perfect."

Lyall dipped his head in a blush.

Biffy felt a heady rush at the power of that. Something so simple as one word of praise to build allegiance. "Shall we head down to face the nappies, as it were?"

"Lead on, Alpha, do."

CHAPTER FIVE

Decorating for Christmas

The drawing room was only slightly less chaotic than it had been the evening before. Apparently, the pack had no intention of keeping their new additions confined to the safe anonymity of the upstairs nursery.

Despite the fact that, under ordinary circumstances, everyone ought to be at breakfast, the pack were all in the drawing room with Mrs Whybrew and the (now three) babies. Quite apart from everything else, this was startling because werewolves, as a rule, never missed a meal.

Well, to be fair, Channing was eating with the clavigers. But no one thought it was a good idea to invite him along at the best of times. To anything. For any reason. Let alone a room full of infants.

Lyall went to speak with said clavigers, while Biffy went to supervise the rest of the pack.

Hemming and Rafe were on the floor, playing with an infant apiece.

Their newest addition was of the walking variety of child, if the odd I'm-about-to-fall waddle was anything to go by. She, and Biffy had to take it on faith that *she* was a *she* because there were no other indicators, could move remarkably fast for someone who clearly hadn't been doing it for very long. The toddler's mode of locomotion had Biffy legitimately worried over the efficaciousness of bipedal motion in future generations.

Quinn was chasing after her, his quizzical brow lined even more than usual. Apparently, he was terrified that she would fall (a legitimate concern with gravity around), or bump into something (which, given the state of one of Biffy's Wedgwood urns, had already occurred).

Biffy looked with mixed feelings upon the urn. It had once been a Westmoreland opal milk glass fluted vase with flower details, imported at great expense and with much fanfare by a certain blond vampire for Biffy's fortieth birthday. It was, however, more to Lord Akeldama's taste than his own. But one did not reject a gift from a vampire – quite apart from anything else, such trinkets were often priceless. *Well, no use crying over spilled milk glass. Ha-ha.*

Biffy stuck his head back out into the hallway and yelled for the butler.

Rumpet the Second rushed up.

Rumpet the Second was a second cousin to the pack's previous butler, Rumpet the Original. Or possibly Premier Rumpet, if one was feeling Roman about one's butlers. Rumpet the Original had retired happily some ten years earlier, on a generous stipend, to a small hamlet called Merkin-on-Tow, or Smirkall-near-Boot or some such rot, where he had become rather well known for his prize chrysanthemums. Every year, he sent the pack a large bunch of his own variant, called the Scarlet Moon. Which Biffy appreciated even if the flowers were most decidedly not scarlet, but more a kind of puce.

Their new Rumpet had arrived shortly after the first batch of chrysanthemums, on his cousin's recommendation, proving himself to look and act remarkably like the first Rumpet, only younger and slightly larger and sporting a pencil-thin mustache. He was occasionally referred to by Adelphus (who thought rather too much of his own wit) as *Rumpet Revisited.*

Regardless of moniker, he was an excellent butler (despite the unfortunate mustache) who had seen them through Alpha transition and subsequent relocation with the unflappably stiff demeanor upon which they had all come to rely. Biffy had even learned to tolerate the mustache. Rumpet had been visiting a sick aunt the evening prior, but was apparently now caught up on the particulars of their involuntary multiple paternity, if his long-suffering expression was anything to go by.

"Ah, Rumpet. Be a good man and have one of the maids clean up the broken glass in our drawing room, if you would be so kind."

"More broken, my lord? Right away, sir."

"And we'd better clear out or elevate the other valuables in the room. If it is to be used for the entertainment of children..." Biffy allowed his displeasure to show.

Rumpet quite agreed with this unspoken commentary on the misuse of a perfectly civilized drawing room. His own eyebrow was minutely elevated in judgment. "Sir."

"We must allow them their fun."

"If you say so, sir." Rumpet slipped off to see about maids and anti-child drawing room fortifications, and Biffy turned back to the scene before him.

Phelan, Zev, and Ulric were off to one side in the

position of commentator, observer, and judge respectively, but they seemed more entertained here than Biffy had ever seen them at the theater.

Biffy took a breath. "What on earth?"

"Alpha!" said Adelphus, "We got landed with another one."

"So I see."

"Same exact style as last time. Simply wrapped in a blanket on the step, poor little lady." Phelan, bless him, seemed to be willing to provide details.

"This one doesn't spit up near as much as the other," added Ulric.

"Thank heavens for small mercies." Zev raised a palm upwards reverently.

"She seems recovered from her ordeal." Biffy did not let any emotion color his tone. Merely made a show of watching the toddler gyrate about the room.

"She has a lot of energy," said Quinn fervently as he chased after. "We thought we'd run it out of her."

"Oh, we did, did we?" Biffy crossed his arms and leaned against the doorjamb. No doubt any one of them could catch the little girl if needed – after all, they were supernaturally fast.

At which juncture the toddler in question dashed past Biffy and out into the hallway, where she crashed into the legs of Major Channing, who was collecting his hat from his claviger and preparing to depart for BUR.

Everyone gasped.

Channing looked down. Very far down. Channing was one of the tallest in the pack.

"Yes?" He frowned at the infant. Channing had, under most circumstances, a decidedly overwhelming effect on females of all species. Until he opened his mouth, of course.

Mrs Whybrew, who'd followed the child to the doorway, stood with her hand to her mouth and her gaze fixed on, most likely, one of the best-looking men she'd ever seen. Or would ever see.

Biffy swiveled to watch but did not relax his stance.

The toddler stopped and stared up, transfixed.

Frankly, Biffy could understand the sentiment. Channing was incredibly easy on the eyes. Lanky but muscled, with crystal-clear blue eyes and pale blond hair. He was like some winter god, Jack Frost perhaps.

If only he didn't also shoot first in the firing squad of premier pompous twats.

"Oh, my heavens," breathed Mrs Whybrew.

It was likely everyone expected Channing to shake the child off his leg in the manner in which one dismisses a tiny dog or a shoe full of rocks.

Biffy was prepared to intervene, as Alpha, if the man turned violent. Channing was difficult at the best of times, and didn't particularly like to be touched, not even by his ladybirds. (Biffy preferred not to contemplate how that even worked.)

The toddler was now clinging to Channing's well-pressed trouser leg, wrinkling it something awful, and there was a good chance sticky finger smudges were also being transferred. (If Biffy knew anything about children, which he did.)

Channing bent down.

The pack held its collective breath.

Biffy relaxed his arms and prepared to shift and strike, or simply place himself in front of a blow. He was, after all, immortal, and he could take the hit.

He could also take Channing, for all the pack Gamma

outweighed him by half again as much.

But Channing only slid two fingers through the little girl's mop of curly red hair.

A look of profound pain crossed Channing's impassively beautiful face but was gone again so quickly, Biffy wondered if it were a trick of the gas lighting. Or if he had imagined it.

Before anything else could happen, Biffy reached down and scooped the child up, carrying her back inside the drawing room.

Channing left, the front door closing quietly behind him.

Biffy said to the recovering Mrs Whybrew, "It would be best to keep the children away from Major Channing, if at all possible. He is a busy man. In fact, might we avoid the hallways as a general rule? And now, if you wouldn't mind taking the three in hand, madam? My pack requires feeding and a few words on standards of behavior appropriate to drawing rooms, it would seem."

He gave what he hoped was a commanding look at the men standing, sitting, and, in the case of Hemming, crawling about the room.

"We are all late for our breakfast. The clavigers have already had theirs. If you would, gentlemen? I require tea." He turned away, hoping they would follow him.

They did.

Biffy must have said something cutting, because Lyall looked up, shortly after Channing left, to see the rest of the pack troop into breakfast without babies and with very cowed expressions.

Lyall didn't think this was the result of any serious discipline. For one thing, no one was bruised or bleeding. For another, Biffy wasn't that kind of Alpha. *Thank heavens.*

Said Alpha seemed more resigned than tense. Lyall hoped Biffy was prepared to stick faithfully to the plan they'd concocted over cravat-tying earlier.

Lyall resisted touching the beautiful knot at his own throat. He certainly wasn't thinking about those long, fine fingers caressing his neck. *Not thinking about it at all.*

Lyall turned his attention, very thoroughly, to his breakfast kippers and dried sprats.

Rumpet the Second had somehow known, with that instinct of all good butlers, that Lyall was one of those rare werewolves who preferred fish. Most were of the sausage and bacon persuasion. *Well,* thought Lyall, amused at his own whimsy, *I've always been one for both sausage and fish. As the saying goes. But at breakfast – kippers.* Perhaps the previous Rumpet had told the new one of his eccentricity. Or perhaps there was such a thing as a collective butler memory for such niceties. Regardless, a generous helping of kippers had been placed before Lyall's seat along with a most excellent pot of tea.

Not for the first time, Lyall marveled at the fine line between butler and Beta.

Lyall sipped his tea reverently. *My, but I missed good British brew,*

The subdued silence didn't last, because the requisite mounds of sausages, slabs of ham, boiled eggs, rump steak pie, and rolled tongue soon distracted the pack from prior chastisement and encouraged conversation in the way that hearty food often does, after an initial pause to inhale first.

The dialogue focused mainly on their newest additions, as might be expected. Lyall decided to let the pack hash things out for a bit before encouraging his Alpha to lay down the letter of the law.

Biffy seemed to agree with this approach. The Alpha sat back and sipped his own tea while the pack got ever more excited around him.

Lyall worried Biffy wasn't eating enough. He offered him the platter of kippers.

Biffy gave him a funny look.

Adelphus started them off in a roundabout way by clearing his throat and announcing, "I believe we must acquire a *Christmas tree*. You know, of the kind that Queen Victoria always insists upon. As the Germans have it."

"Why on earth?" Biffy wanted to know.

"It's what people with children do," Adelphus told his boiled egg firmly, not quite able to look Biffy in the eye.

"Oh, is it indeed?" Biffy was not going to make this easy on them.

"Of course it is. Makes the place more homey." Hemming grinned.

"And smell nice." Quinn was hopeful.

"Oh! We could put evergreen boughs all down the banisters. Saw that done at a ball once, very festive." Hemming's blue eyes started to shine with enthusiasm.

"Indeed? I don't recall any of you so keen to decorate when it was curtains and carpets." Biffy arched his eyebrows. But Lyall could tell that the Alpha was being playful, not critical.

As if Biffy will ever brook interference from this pack

on the matter of interior decorating. The choice of purple curtains alone shows he did not consult with them. Very daring, given our already contentious vampire relations.

"Should we mull cider?" asked Rafe. "Or maybe have Cook mull cider? Should I ask Rumpet? Rumpet would know. Rumpet!"

"Wassail?" suggested Ulric.

"Do humans still brew wassail?" Zev frowned.

"Aren't cider and wassail the same thing?" That was Phelan, under his breath in genuine confusion, looking at Lyall. The moniker "Professor" meant most of the pack turned to the Beta in times of verbal or cultural confusion, despite the fact that his particular area of expertise was in the procreative habits of *Ovis aries*. Not, as Phelan seemed to currently believe, the finer niceties of hot, fruity seasonal beverages.

"Is *brewing* even the right word? I thought wassail was… sort of… steeped." Quinn stabbed a sausage thoughtfully.

"Like tea?" Adelphus sipped his.

"Sirs?" Rumpet slid into the room.

"Rumpet, please see if you can lay on some wassail, or maybe hot cider," instructed Rafe. "Or possibly that wine they do with the spices. What's it called?"

"Sir?" Rumpet looked in confusion at Biffy.

Biffy shook his head a little and rolled his eyes.

"For the children, Rumpet," explained Adelphus, as if this should be perfectly obvious.

The unflappable Rumpet appeared rather flapped at that statement. "But sir! I'm tolerably certain infants should not imbibe beverages of the inebriatory variety. Terribly bad for the constitution."

"Oh, not to drink, my man, simply to make the place

smell nice." Rafe's brown eyes crinkled in amusement.

Feeling that this was unfair on the butler and tantamount to teasing the household staff, which was the very height of rudeness, Lyall was moved to interject, "Perhaps you and the servants would like to partake yourselves?"

Rumpet gave him a grateful look. "If you insist, sir, that's very thoughtful and festively minded of you. But I shouldn't like it to become a habit."

"Oh, Rumpet, don't be silly, this is only for the holidays." Zev seemed on board with the general scheme to festoon the household in vegetative matter and fermented-fruit smells.

Lyall was pleased to see him engaged. Zev had confessed that he'd been feeling a little forlorn of late. Apparently, the idea of holiday celebrations cheered up everyone, even werewolves.

"And there's always the clavigers, they'll drink anything." Adelphus pointed out the obvious.

Actors.

Rumpet looked mollified but no less confused.

"And we'll need evergreens as well," said Rafe. "Maybe even a tree."

Rumpet's mouth twisted. "That's awfully *European*, sir."

"And what about a Yule log?" Ulric added.

"For the nippers. Think of the nippers." Hemming again.

"It's your drawing room, sirs."

Biffy stood at this juncture, which meant everyone else fell silent.

Rumpet looked grateful.

Lyall could almost hear him thinking, *Finally, a voice*

of reason.

"Why don't we go easy for now, Rumpet? Just some spiced and roasted apples for the pudding course at supper later tonight – that will help make the house smell nice. The evergreen boughs seem like a good idea regardless, something to celebrate the season. I'll collect some ribbon to tie them up with, from the hat shop."

Lyall smiled to himself. For certainly Biffy would never let anyone else choose the color of ribbons meant to drape over his banisters.

"For the rest, we shall see how things lie next week, hum? It's not Christmas yet, after all. Thank you for your time, Rumpet. Perhaps a little more tea?"

Relieved that things had been made clear by the Alpha, Rumpet bowed. "Certainly, my lord. Right away." He practically dashed from the room.

"Are we keeping them? I think we should keep them." Hemming finished his breakfast and pushed the plate away so he could lean forward intently on his elbows, blue eyes pleading.

Lyall considered reprimanding him for posture. But really, why bother? Hemming wasn't going to change the habit of two lifetimes.

Biffy arched a perfect brow. "Keeping the pine boughs? Of course we are. Well, until they dry out."

"The nippers!" said Hemming.

"Please, Alpha, can't we keep them? They're so cute!" Quinn tried to look and sound winsome. On a quizzically browed six-foot-plus werewolf, this was as odd as a snake wearing shoes.

Biffy rolled his eyes. "We can't simply keep two babies, even if someone did leave them on our doorstep."

A chorus of *why not*s met that statement.

Biffy's eyes narrowed. "It's not done. And I'll hear no more on it!"

Crestfallen looks all around. Even from Ulric, whom Lyall had thought aloof in the matter of infant impositions.

Lyall sighed, and went to provide support, like any good Beta. "See here, gentlemen. They must belong to someone, you understand? They need to be returned to their rightful owners, or what have you."

In an effort to move them on, he added, "The Alpha and I have discussed this matter" – a slight inclination of Biffy's head and Lyall continued – "and we feel it necessary to spend tonight hunting for the parental relations. Most of you can be spared from your regular duties for one night. I've drawn up a list of places around Greenwich worthy of our attention. Also, I think it best if two of us attend service this evening. It had better be you, Adelphus and Phelan."

Lyall chose them because, quite frankly, they cut the best leg and were the most toff of the pack. Adelphus could come over too arrogant, but he looked a fine dandy in his Sunday best, and was almost regal when sitting in a pew.

Lyall might be recently returned to London, but he'd decades with this pack under other Alphas, and both Adelphus and Phelan knew (without his having to tell them) why they'd been chosen to pray first.

"If you can, after, try to track down this other religious group that the pastor was muttering about? I want the lay of the land. How they react to you two, as werewolves, will give a good indication of general attitude. Let's hope we aren't dealing with one of those militant types that likes to stand on top of pulpits and throw things. So unseemly. If we have a Dark Ages issue, or worse, some kind of Sundower sympathizers, better we know it now."

Looking slightly more grave, the two nodded.

Lyall continued. "Hemming and Rafe, you're touring the taverns and pubs. I know, quite the hardship. But try to remember we are after information. Anything pertaining to missing children. Any other abandoned infants turning up? Or is it just *our* doorstep? Ask after the history of this house. Perhaps it used to be an orphanage or hospital or charitable organization before we moved in.

"Quinn, I've got you down for tradesmen and the like. Grocers, butchers, and so forth. Ask Cook who has our accounts, visit them first. Then do the others. Wave the carrot of a possible switch to encourage goodwill. Ulric, you're on the high-end stuff, jewelers, pawn shops, dressmakers. Remember we're after information, not pocket watches. No, you can't draw on the pack accounts, so don't bother to ask. And Zev, you know where that leaves you?"

Zev nodded, smiling. "Entertainment, in all its many forms."

"Well, don't go wild. Our clavigers have the local musical halls and theaters covered, but there are other forms of amusement. Gaming hells, brothels, molly houses."

Zev had a sweet boyish face, open and honest and clean-shaven with big dark eyes and outrageous lashes. He could use it all to very good effect, particularly the lashes. As a result, he was remarkably effective in the worst parts of London.

Biffy's lip curled. "Really, Professor, we are in Greenwich, not Bethnal Green!"

Lyall gave him a blank, unconcerned look. Knowing the Alpha found this annoying. Well, mostly he found it annoying – once, he had found it something more. A temptation and a taunt. *I simply want to ruffle you up, Alpha, disturb you, make you feel something.* "There are still docks here, Alpha. And we don't have Riehard."

Biffy relented. "Curse the man. The one time we really do need his particular brand of assistance."

Lyall nodded. "When is he due back, again?" This question was directed at the pack, since Riehard had left before Lyall returned.

"Should be within the next few days," volunteered Zev. "You know he doesn't like to be away for more than two weeks, and always returns before full moon."

Biffy nodded. "As he should."

Riehard was their most elusive pack-mate. Lyall had once wondered why he even bothered with a pack at all. Until Lyall realized, with the life Riehard Tiklebark led, he needed the pack more than most. More than Channing, more than Biffy – *more, even, than I.* Riehard was tethered so loosely to reality, he needed a strong tether to an Alpha or he would drift and become a danger to society and himself. Lyall hoped fervently that Biffy could hold him. Riehard was many things – redhead, blond, and brunet in the space of one evening, for example – but he was also an asset.

But for now, they would have to hunt without him.

Biffy tilted his head at Lyall. "And what of you and I, my Beta?"

Lyall suppressed a smile at the claiming tone. "Visiting hours, I'm afraid, with the local gentry."

"Oh, really, must we?"

"Not *we*, my lord. I believe someone requested my

nose on this job."

Biffy nodded with only a slight roll of his eyes.

Later, as they all parted ways in the hallway, Lyall turned away from the others to return to his quarters to strip and change shape. His nose was good in both forms, but better as a wolf.

Biffy stopped him with a gentle touch to his neck above his collar. "Pity. I put so much care into this knot."

Lyall let himself love, for one brief moment, the soft caress, and then fled upstairs. He almost welcomed the pain of the shift, for it might distract from the pain of his memories.

Lyall sniffed the swaddling clothes of both infants. Nothing particularly unique stood out from the expected scent of human nursling, except that they were not at all similar. Wherever the children had originated, it wasn't the same household, or workhouse, or orphanage.

So, Lyall took a deep breath of Robin's blanket, stuck his nose to the cold wet street, and ran out into the night.

He had absolutely no luck with that trail – it stopped close to the pack house at a nearby street corner in a mess of horse and leather. No doubt the infant had arrived by carriage.

That in and of itself was interesting, as it meant whoever brought him had more money than one might expect from someone bent on abandoning a child. Robin had not, therefore, been *abandoned,* but instead *intentionally delivered.*

The redheaded toddler, whom, for lack of another option, they were calling Rosie, had a longer scent trail.

Hers went well towards the main village of Blackheath, which was a good sign, as it meant she might be local. If she'd originated in London central, finding her relations could be well-nigh impossible.

Lyall spent the next few hours in fur. He was small for a wolf, lean and vulpine. He faded easily into the background shadows, dismissed more often as a stray dog or very large fox than a fearsome werewolf.

He paced the streets of the middle classes first, sniffing for anything that might remind him of the scent of either child. Then he went to the poorer alleys and waysides.

He thought, at one point, that he caught a whiff of Rosie at an abandoned warehouse, but there was no one there and nobody inside. Still, he made note of the location, as it might be worth setting a claviger to watch the place come daylight.

CHAPTER SIX

A Crisis of Nasal Proportions

Biffy really wished he had Riehard in residence. No doubt that particular werewolf would have nipped down to the Crown and Sceptre and returned a few hours later with all their questions answered. Biffy and Riehard had always gotten along well. Riehard had a gift for gathering information and Biffy had a gift for loving it. Some might call Biffy a gossip, but only lesser intellects.

Without Riehard, Biffy had to put his faith in Rafe – a shaky proposition. Oh, he knew why Lyall had chosen Rafe and Hemming for pub detail. Hemming was for jocularity and show. And Rafe was for appearances. Rafe was their most (frankly) common-looking pack mate. He had a rough-and-tumble air not helped by the fact that he'd been metamorphosed with two days' worth of beard and no inclination to fix it. It gave him, Biffy felt, a sadly plebeian aura. Rafe wasn't as good as Richard ut extracting information, because he tended to come over friendly and start singing bawdy tunes and lose track of things. But he was better than nothing, so Biffy waved him off to the pub, resigned to the fact that at least it wasn't Channing. Channing never did anyone any favors at pubs.

Then Biffy's own trials must commence.

Visiting the gentry was a necessary evil that he'd already conducted the day after moving. Biffy was no slouch where the observation of proper etiquette was concerned. The rules were very strict on the matter of a lord taking up residence in a new neighborhood. The fact that said lordling came complete with a pack of werewolves was neither here nor there to the necessity of paying calls. So, calls he had paid. All of them.

The gentry of Blackheath proved itself by and large to be the type to have opted for Greenwich over North London. Which is to say, more relaxed and also a great deal less fashionable than was Biffy's routine society. They had a great deal more concern for the state of the whitebait fisheries than for the arrangement of their hair. Biffy tried not to hold this against them. *Although, really, how hard is it to find yourself a decent barber once a month? One must forgive both the sins of the fish and flesh, I suppose, when living in Greenwich.* Needless to say, he did not relish the idea of having to pay another round of calls again so soon.

Nevertheless, he did as Lyall bid – making polite inquiries that might lead the various mildly confused ladies and gentlemen (or better, their staff) to mention the unexpected absence of a child from their household.

Nothing.

He returned to the house for midnight dinner to find the others equally fruitless and the babies in question abed. Thank heavens Mrs Whybrew seemed to feel it best to keep them to a daylight schedule, despite being fostered by a pack of werewolves.

Dinner was eaten in ravenous silence and then filled with reports on what had not been found. After this, the pack split again and went back on the hunt.

Visiting hours had ended and there were no balls or parties Biffy might attend. So, he and Lyall joined forces to amble about the town, not really hoping for anything, just as something to do.

"That warehouse where you think you caught the scent, will you show me?"

Lyall nodded.

It was a quiet, companionable walk. This was something Biffy had always liked about Lyall. He could make civilized conversation with the best of them, but when he had nothing to say, he said nothing.

Biffy couldn't help but notice, however, that the good professor wore his greatcoat buttoned all the way up to the throat. Which meant it was likely he wore nothing underneath. Biffy tried to be more worried than intrigued. As a rule, if a werewolf had limited control over his wolf form, he might opt for less clothing over more on any given evening, in case of shift. But Professor Lyall was noted for his control, so the greatcoat meant that Lyall was anticipating trouble.

This was something to which it had taken Biffy nearly a decade to acclimate. Knowing that the gentleman next to you was, essentially, naked could play hell with the sensibilities of any dandy, let alone one who rather fancied the nude male form. Biffy had learned to manage it with equanimity. But now he realized he was not yet there when it came to *Professor Lyall's* nude male form.

They arrived at the warehouse in question, and Lyall proved himself unexpectedly adept with a lock pick. Inside, the place was entirely empty and cleaner than one might expect, with a raised platform at one end, like a small stage of some kind.

They sniffed about, but the scents were muddled and the place too plain to offer much beyond smells in the way of information. Although Professor Lyall had a good eye.

"It does appear that a group is assembling here regularly. See there, the mark of a door recently and frequently pushed open?" Lyall gestured to scrape marks on the dirt floor.

Biffy investigated the small stage. It smelled heavily of vinegar, obvious even to his inferior human olfactory sense. *Perhaps this place was previously used for pickling operations? Or a cider press?* "After-hours bawdy theater?" he suggested.

"Perhaps a political gathering place?" Lyall stood back and watched while Biffy took to the stage.

Biffy grinned. "As if there's a difference."

Professor Lyall gave a quiet chuckle.

Finding nothing of interest, Biffy jumped down and rejoined his Beta. "I can't really spare anyone right now, but I'll set someone to watch the place during the day tomorrow."

Lyall frowned. "What do you mean, *can't spare anyone?*"

Biffy winced. *Admission time.* He hated to be humiliated in Lyall's estimation, but it wouldn't do to have a Beta out of the loop either.

"You met with the clavigers earlier this evening."

Lyall nodded.

"Not very many of them, are there?" Biffy kept his expression blank.

They walked out of the warehouse.

Lyall locked the door after them, fine hands nimble with the heavy bolt. "Half dozen? I assumed some had already left about their business." He wiped down the metal with a handkerchief and a bit of lemon oil from a vial in his coat pocket.

Smart. Lemon to disguise the musk of wolf. "No more than six."

They headed back towards the new pack house.

There was a long pause while Lyall contemplated numbers and, no doubt, how to ask the obvious question politely. When he finally got around to it, his voice was soft and kind. "Why so few, Alpha?"

Biffy looked at his hands. Once so fine and clean and gloved. He never wore gloves anymore, and his knuckles always seemed to be smudged or scratched. "No new petitions since I took charge, and we lost over half when Lord Maccon retired."

"But they know you have Anubis Form?"

Biffy nodded, miserable. How humiliating had that been? To have to show the assembled clavigers that he was capable of making new werewolves. To prove himself with that grotesque wolf's head on a human body.

He whispered it to his hands. "They still left. I couldn't hold them."

Lyall gave him an unreadable look. "Their loss."

Biffy stayed silent.

A gentle hand to his wrist stopped him in the street.

"You're afraid the pack will start to abandon you, like the clavigers did?"

Biffy said nothing, only lowered his eyes. *I have one job to do now. One charge. Them. Hold them together. Keep them sane. How can I keep my wolves when I can't even keep my humans?*

Lyall's voice was low and urgent. "This pack has been through this before – transitioning Alphas. Well, most of us have. The Alpha isn't all that holds us together, we also legitimately like each other. We're family. Mostly."

"And I'm like the evil step-wolf from some contorted fairy tale."

Lyall gave a small tight smile. "Which one of us is Snow White?"

"Ulric, of course. Zev is the little matchstick girl."

Lyall chuckled. "And who is Sleeping Beauty?"

This was kind of a fun game. "Definitely Channing. We all live in hope some day he'll wake up and grow a personality."

Lyall nodded. "And Cinderella?"

Biffy looked away. "You of course, professor." *Always running after dust mites and putting things to rights. Always tidying the world around you to exacting specifications. Always wishing for something more.* Then, before Lyall could grow uncomfortable, he added, "There have been no formal applications, Lyall. Not a single one. The clavigers we do have were recruits. They're all after patronage, not immortality. No one trusts me to metamorphose them successfully."

"Or perhaps London has changed and immortality has lost its luster?" Lyall was trying to be kind.

Biffy shook his head. He couldn't believe that. Surely, other Alphas had clavigers who wanted to try for bite. "It's me, the way I look, the way I am. No one trusts me to be a strong Alpha."

Lyall closed his eyes and shook his head. "Fools, to judge so much by appearances. You developed Anubis Form early. And you have always shifted forms quickly.

And you fight smart. Those are true signs of Alpha strength. Not to be diminished by the fact that your collar points are high and your waistcoats tight."

"Judge not the werewolf by the starch of his apparel but by the speed of its removal?" Biffy suggested.

Lyall chuckled. As he was supposed to.

Biffy returned to being serious. "It's not easy with only six clavigers. I've been thinking of hiring more footmen and a valet or two. I mean to say, Riehard doesn't need anyone, but we should really pay someone to put up with Channing, Adelphus, Ulric, and, well, me. We're a bit too demanding for clavigers."

Lyall nodded. "I noticed some of the pack were dressing far better than when I left. Your influence?"

"I believe it's more that my presence gives them permission. Ulric now openly reads the Paris fashion papers. Last week, Phelan and Channing actually got into an argument about the old-fashioned nature of a mathematical cravat tie. Not that the others haven't struggled to improve themselves as well under my guidance." *And occasional prodding.*

"An Alpha leads by example and you care deeply about appearances."

"I do."

"Perhaps that's why some of the clavigers left."

"They think me shallow?"

"No, they no longer fit with the pack. Or no longer felt that they did."

Alpha and Beta had reached the front door of their new home at this juncture. Biffy pushed inside the house, uncomfortable with continuing this conversation where others might overhear. But knowing, now that he'd started, he must tell Lyall everything and unburden himself of all his flaws.

The butler rushed forward to take their coats. Well, Biffy's coat. Taking Lyall's wouldn't be politic.

"Rumpet, bring two large glasses of brandy up to my chambers, please. Professor Lyall and I have pack business to discuss. We are not to be disturbed." If he talked quietly and quickly inside the confines of his own bedroom, the servants wouldn't be able to eavesdrop. A werewolf likely could, but the rest of the pack was still out hunting.

Lyall didn't seem concerned by the intimacy of the invitation. Likely, he understood the need for discretion rather than any possible implication of indiscretion.

Nevertheless, Biffy self-consciously waited while his guest selected a seat in his private quarters. He was oddly crushed when Lyall opted for the chair next to the fireplace rather than the small settee in front of it. Apparently, Lyall was ensuring that they not share a piece of furniture.

His Beta sat and sipped his brandy. Waiting.

Biffy took the settee, lifted his own glass, and stared contemplatively at the amber liquid within.

Biffy liked his room well enough to live in it, although it was not what he once might have wished. Its appearance was all compromise, balance between his very exacting standards and his animalistic nature. He'd found, once a werewolf, that a certain inherent clumsiness in human form (regardless of the possibility of becoming a lunatic beast) was disastrous to delicate furniture. Fine spindly legs and fussy details were simply not werewolf-compatible. It was as though, while he had not grown more muscle, he had lost some gracefulness of form and replaced it with concentrated strength. His bones and tendons were more solid and stiff. Forced to rely upon heavy thick chairs, solid stable tables, and wrought iron, Biffy strove to balance this clunkiness with delicacy in the matter of light, airy curtains and cream upholstery. His bedroom was, therefore, an exercise in contradictions. His dark chairs and tables were solid mahogany but beautifully carved and rounded wherever possible, glassy with polish, and spread with filmy muslin cloth. His settee was low and stable and made of thick, resilient velvet, but in an elegant pale sage color.

No doubt Lyall saw all these differing elements, took them in through those measuring hazel eyes. Certainly, his Beta assessed them with that wickedly sharp mind and saw that part of Biffy that was at war with himself. The solid iron bed, its circular decorative elements more like gears or compasses than flowers, the canopy over the head taller and wider than any human would require. The bed coverlet was velvet again, striped cream and gold, but chosen with durability in mind rather than warmth. Biffy no longer needed warmth, and though he rarely slept *well*, he was still a werewolf – during daylight, he always slept *solid*.

It is all the pretty things that I wanted, draped over all the durable and ugly things that I have become.

"So," said Lyall at last. "Tell me, Alpha."

"Alpha?"

A small huff of amusement met that. "Tell me, Biffy."

"I can't hold them together. Whatever is needed of an Alpha, I don't think I have enough of it. They're always arguing with me. They don't trust my judgment. It's no wonder the claviers left me. Without them, I feel like the pack trusts me even less. I'm too young, too new at this. Don't most Alphas spend decades as loners first?"

"You are not the type of man to be a loner."

"No, I'm not." *I'd never survive. Not that I couldn't fight. Simply that I'd have nothing to fight for. Perhaps that's part of this as well. I'm afraid that I need the pack more than the pack needs me.* Biffy drank the last of his brandy. It burned his throat but did nothing more. The comforting looseness of intoxication was no longer an option. Well, there was formaldehyde – drink enough of that and even a werewolf turned squiffy. But the last thing he needed as a few-months-old Alpha was to lose control.

Lyall put his still-full brandy glass down on the table between them. Then in one of those lightning-quick movements that Biffy had learned to anticipate from the supernatural set, Lyall shifted to sit next to him on the settee.

I forgot he could move so fast. Much of Lyall's survival and his fighting skills came from his speed. Lord Maccon once said he knew of none faster, and that had Professor Lyall been a big enough wolf, and of the right temperament, he would have been the foremost Alpha in the land. But, of course, Lyall was neither. So, his speed was made to serve a pack, and serve them it had for hundreds of years.

Biffy knew agility was some of his own Alpha skill set as well. As if by swindling them both in the size department when compared to other werewolves, the gods of immortality had deemed Biffy and Lyall worthy of great speed and cunning instead. So far, Biffy had only had to fight a few times, but he practiced a lot. He'd decided, after defeating Channing, he'd take what he'd been given and learn to use it. *Perhaps Lyall can teach me some of his tricks.*

Lyall moved closer until they were almost touching, side by side on the small couch. Both of them watched the play of the fire rather than each other.

Biffy turned his gaze, almost desperately, to his empty glass.

Lyall reached out and took it out of his hands, setting it aside.

Then those fine gentle fingers were pressing insistently on Biffy's cheek, turning his head, tilting Biffy's face until he was forced to look into serious sand-colored eyes.

Sad eyes. Always. Even when Lyall was smiling, or plotting, or fighting, or solving some pack riddle or another, his eyes were always a little sad. Only a few times had Biffy seen them wide and full of wonder, almost but not quite joyful. *And I most certainly shouldn't be thinking about that right now, with my bed right there.*

Biffy lowered his eyelashes, collected himself. He recounted the twenty perfect cravat knots in his head. He contemplated the button choices he'd been offered for his next waistcoat. *I think I'll go with the milk glass. I should have James contact my tailor with that decision.* He collected himself.

Lyall's fingers did not stroke Biffy's skin – there was no caress to his touch, only insistence and comfort.

"Tell me."

Biffy stayed silent and turned his face into the hand, seeking more. It instantly withdrew.

Biffy flinched. "I was rather hoping you could tell me." *He does not want me anymore. Not in that way.*

Lyall sighed. He pushed Biffy back against the corner of the settee and then turned himself around and rested against him. His back was lean and warm on Biffy's chest.

It was a pose of lovers. A way they had sat in the past. Only, they were both dressed, and this felt more like friendship and necessary intimacy than lust.

Biffy took it, though. He was embarrassingly grateful for whatever scraps he was offered. He held Lyall close, but not tightly, and tried not to breathe in his scent. Not because he didn't want to – because he *did* want to. Too much. Lyall clearly did not desire that. Did not desire him. Oh, but it wasn't easy.

Lyall was offering him comfort without obligation, and connection without expectation. He had arranged them to be close but only so that Biffy would not have to look directly at him while he confessed his deficiencies. No Alpha could bear that, to look into sympathetic eyes.

He knows I am crumbling and he wants to help. He knows it is now impossible for me to expose any deficiency. He is making it so I can do so with support but not confrontation.

Biffy wondered if Lyall had done this for any of his previous Alphas. No doubt Biffy was not so different from them in matters of guilt and confession. *If I was made to lead and to take risks with my actions, my greatest fear, by default, must be failure. Well, that and any change that I myself have not chosen.*

I guess I really am an Alpha.

So, Biffy held his love against him, not too tight. And encouraged into release by his Beta's easy acceptance, Biffy spoke of all the terrors of the young and responsible when the weight of a broken dream is upon them.

Lyall lay motionless in his Alpha's undemanding embrace. He had instigated it, but Biffy had not repelled him. Unfortunately, he had not drawn him closer, either. His Alpha's hands, laced together, rested open and still and undemanding on Lyall's chest.

He needs to tell me what's wrong. He needs to articulate all of it so that I can understand and help. Lyall waited, keeping his breath even.

He has the charisma to hold this pack. There's no reason the clavigers should have left us. Unless it is that they can sense how he doubts himself.

Lyall could tell that Biffy needed many things from him. But principally, he needed guidance towards a better understanding of Alpha nature and pack structure. Only then could they come up with a cure for this thing that was eating away at what was left of Biffy's soul. The other need, Lyall's own, a temptation that was dormant beneath everything, would only complicate matters. *I had forgotten the way his lips curved, and that his bottom one is slightly fuller than the top.*

What we had was just the one moment to help us both overcome loss, him of his past and me of my future. I cannot encumber him with the awkwardness of my continued desire. It's not fair. Another requirement for an overburdened Alpha. Another need to fulfill.

Lyall did many things, but he never, ever imposed. *What was comfort is now friendship. And that is good enough. It must be good enough.*

Finally, Biffy began to speak. "They went mad at the end there. All of them, not only Lord Maccon. He refused to leave, you see, even though we all knew it was time. And I..." Biffy's voice broke a moment. "I *liked* him. He was my Alpha. My friend. But he wasn't here anymore, not present, there was just the shell of him left."

Lyall explained, "He was losing his tethers."

"Vampires are tethered to place, werewolves to pack." Biffy repeated the old saying.

But did he really understand it? Had Conall been well enough to give him that much training? When Lyall left, he'd thought Lord Maccon was still holding everything together. He'd thought, with Lady Maccon's particular abilities, that they could weather Alpha curse and come out the better for it. *Perhaps I was wrong.*

So, Lyall felt it his duty to ensure Biffy knew now. "It's not simply a platitude. When you became Alpha of this pack, you tethered to them, to each and every member. Your tether is the last of your soul, so, in a way, the pack *becomes* the Alpha's soul. And you are theirs."

"And what about you?" Biffy wondered. The slight breath of his speaking shivered over Lyall's hair.

"You didn't feel it snap back into place? In the hat shop, when you knew it was me and I didn't smell right?"

Mine. "Oh. That. You still don't smell quite right."

Of course, Lyall knew how to change that in a hurry. *You could mark me, inside and out. We could... Not a good idea. Continue the lesson.*

"That will change. I'm only just home. Anyway, clavigers aren't pack, they aren't supernatural, they have no sense of tether."

"But the pack could still leave me."

"Perhaps. But it would not be easy. Because they are also tethered to each other."

"This seems awfully tangled up and messy."

Lyall smiled. Now Biffy was looking down at him. "Before Lord Vulkasin... died" – *before I arranged to have him killed* – "the pack had no clavigers left at all.

All of them were dead or had run away."

"Is that where I'm headed?" Biffy knew the story of the previous Lord Woolsey, of the mad Alpha before Lord Maccon, and of Lyall's role in seeing him dispossessed. At least, he knew *some* of the story. Lord Vulkasin had taken Alpha's curse to an extreme, turning violent, cruel, and abusive.

"You have hundreds of years, young pup, before you need face Alpha's curse. I merely tell you so that you realize clavigers come and go. We need them, but they do not need us. Thus, they can leave when times are unsettled."

"Are you saying I need to settle?"

"Yes, I suppose in a way I am. You need to focus on pack, on building our new home together."

"Solidifying my tethers?"

"Exactly. Stability. Loyalty. Then everything else will follow."

"How do I do that? The rest of the pack... they are all so much older and stronger than I am."

"When you were with Lord Akeldama, you were, without question, leader of his drones. How did that happen? How did all those young men come to look to you for guidance? You were no older than they, nor were you physically stronger, nor were you better positioned in society. How did Lord Akeldama come to rely upon you? Even the vampire himself leaned on your strength. I saw him do so, more than once."

"I don't know, it simply happened that way. It was easier for me to lead and for the other drones to follow. I was good at making the right decisions and willing to step to the fore. They trusted me. Because, I guess, I trusted them." Biffy shifted under Lyall, a shudder of realization. "Oh."

Lyall twisted to look up at him, to see the understanding in those blue eyes. "So, Alpha?"

"I think I have curtains to replace."

"The purple ones?"

"How did you know? Don't answer that – of course you knew."

Lyall made to shift off of Biffy. Reluctant to lose the contact but knowing his task was done.

Biffy's arms tightened then, slightly. "Not yet, please. A little longer. I haven't been like this with anyone in a long time."

Please from an Alpha. Something to be savored.

Lyall wanted to ask how long. He wanted to know if he had been replaced, and with whom. But he was way too old for such juvenile prying. And whom was he fooling? He didn't want to leave Biffy's arms either. It had been a long time for him as well.

Lyall thought he felt Biffy's head tilt forward, and a tiny feather-light nuzzle against the top of his own. He wanted so badly for it to be real.

But even if it were, how awful to take advantage again? His new Alpha was vulnerable and lonely. He was seeking solace, not love. It would be unfair of Lyall to offer himself under such circumstances, knowing he wanted more than Biffy was capable of giving. Friendship would have to be enough.

I didn't think it would be this difficult.

CHAPTER SEVEN

If Offerings Were Babies

They'd fallen asleep like that. Dozing off. Biffy woke, just before dawn, with a crick in his neck and the weight of his Beta still curled against his chest. Comforting, welcome warmth.

Poor Lyall, he's been traveling forever, and finally arrives home only to find screaming babies and shaken Alphas and a pack in crisis.

Unwilling to lose contact just yet, Biffy slid out from under Lyall, and, blessing his supernatural strength, lifted his Beta and carried him to the bed. Biffy set him, still in his greatcoat, atop the covers. Nothing untoward might be thought of him lying there like that.

Still fully clothed himself, and wincing for the state of his trousers on the morrow, feeling only a little guilty at manipulating Lyall's exhaustion, Biffy crawled next to him on the counterpane.

He didn't curl about him or put his head to the crook of Lyall's shoulder as they had once done so easily – that seemed too much like what they'd been before and were no longer. Instead, Biffy reached out a hand and rested his fingers gently in Lyall's slack palm. Only that small press of touch and familiarity.

He slept the whole day through, untroubled.

When Biffy awoke again, Lyall was gone. As if that weren't bad enough, James came in and attempted to put him in a green tweed suit. *Green. Tweed. In town!* After disabusing him of this notion – *Tweed is for the country and shooting, James, I know Greenwich seems provincial, but it is not the country and I am not currently possessed with the need to shoot anything, except perhaps this suit* – they agreed upon a nice dark blue number instead.

It was a trying start to the evening, only improved upon, in the worst possible way, by the discovery that yet another baby had been left on the pack's doorstep.

Biffy had had enough.

Fortunately, one of the clavigers had been on "doorstep watch" out the front parlor window, and gone running after the departing carriage with Rumpet hot on his heels. (Rumpet because the young man had left without hat or coat, not because butlers worried about baby deposits.) And once the iron fist of Rumpet was released from the household... Most of the clavigers and staff gave chase as well.

The clavigers liked to rise in the late afternoon to get themselves dressed and ready before the pack awoke. Seeing one of their number dash out the door at sunset, followed by Rumpet, meant three others should follow, plus a footman, and the upstairs maid. This left only James and one other claviger to tend the waking pack.

Being that they were mostly dancers, singers, and stage performers, pursuit of a carriage was accompanied by much leaping and bounding, colorful language, and not a few capes, forming a mini herd trailing the offending conveyance down the street. Unfortunately, none of them were of the Greek Olympiad marathon variety (had they been, Lord Akeldama would never have allowed them to move house), so the carriage soon outpaced the mob. They returned home in an excited breathless clatter, to report that while it escaped their clutches, it had sped through Blackheath towards the warehouse district and the docks.

That being a most excellent point of data, Biffy was inclined not to grumble about the pink-cheeked, bright-eyed, hair-mussed return of his underlings. Instead, he praised them for perspicacious action, and listened for any further details that might be of use. He didn't even mock them for the capes. He'd once had a weakness for a nice cape himself when on an escapade.

I wonder if Alphas are permitted capes? Too frivolous? Another vampire-only affectation?

Unfortunately, while the boys had noted the exact style and design of the carriage, not to mention the cut of the coachman's coat and hat, none of this was particularly useful. There was no crest and it was unmarked hired transport, not privately owned and branded. Still, Biffy was pleased. They'd done their very best, and to his standards. Wassail was brought up in gratitude. It proved a most welcome addition.

The second bit of good news came over breakfast, when Adelphus and Phelan commenced chattering on about their research into the new religious sect in the area. They casually mentioned that the group was informal enough not to have consecrated grounds, but instead was reputed to assemble out on the heath when the weather was fine, and in an old warehouse or tent when it was inclement.

This caused poor Ulric no end of distress. "Did you say preaching... outside? How very rough and ready."

"Well, that's the problem, we believe."

Biffy perked up and speared Adelphus with what he hoped was a very crafty look. "What's the problem?"

"The head preacher is reputed to be one of those barn-raisers. Or do I mean tent pole-lifters?"

Biffy quirked a brow. "Do you, Adelphus?"

Adelphus, who had no shame and liked to keep every possible option open, winked. "Not that kind of revival, my dear. Anyway, where was I? Oh, yes, all I am saying is that this man seems the type to climb up on top of things and..." He cleared his throat and looked embarrassed. "...raise his voice."

"How unbecoming," said Phelan.

"How very not on," agreed Hemming.

"Is he English?" wondered Quinn.

"No. All signs point to his being" – a long pregnant pause – "an American."

Silence met that statement. Adelphus basked in everyone's appalled reactions. He had a flair for the dramatic.

"Ah, well, regardless of any possible connection to, you know, our current issue with, well, *human issue*, we will have to investigate further." Lyall didn't look like he was trying to be cute, but he was cute. *Impossibly cute.*

Biffy nodded to show he entirely agreed with his Beta (he would hardly do otherwise at table). He privately wished the American preacher to perdition. He already had four children to provenance, and rogue preachers were quite pushing things too far.

However, *American* meant any rhetoric being shouted (ugh) was likely to be anti-supernatural, and that simply couldn't be allowed to continue. Not by Biffy's pack, and certainly not in England. He would have to deal with this new problem.

I am beginning to very much regret having moved us to Greenwich.

"Very well. Professor Lyall and I discovered a likely warehouse last night. I want a watch set all night tonight and all day tomorrow. If there's anti-supernatural sentiment brewing, that has to be the priority. The accidental children are fine in our keeping for now. I acknowledge that their relations are likely rather worried" – he tilted his head at Hemming's distressed expression – "but they must now play second fiddle to this new inconvenience. If not connected to the children, the cult must be our focus."

The werewolves around the table all agreed.

Channing, who'd remained uncharacteristically silent throughout breakfast, finished his meal and stood.

Biffy gave him a look that he hoped was full of enigmatic wisdom but probably looked more anemic.

Fortunately, Channing tilted his head slightly in supplication. "Yes, I'll stop by on my way to BUR and make inquiries at the Home Office. But this preacher is not registered – I would have known already if he were. I cleared this area before we relocated. He's not official, but I'll ask around to be certain. There are always rabble-rousers and anarchists and the like – Home Office keeps an eye on the known elements."

Biffy nodded. "I'd appreciate it."

Channing's lip curled. "Of course, Alpha." Without another word, he left the table.

Lyall watched him go. "Such a charmer."

Biffy turned back. He couldn't keep all pack from their normal jobs and duties a second night running. Since they'd been relieved of military service overseas, they weren't on strict schedules for tangential military duties, instead working for BUR, serving with Her Majesty's Growlers, or helping out the War Office. Pack business always took priority, but even an American preacher and four squalling babies couldn't be furnished as an excuse for more than one day.

Still, it wasn't all of them. Rafe hadn't any official obligations at the moment. Hemming wanted to stay home and help Mrs Whybrew. She was eminently capable, but four children under a year old was enough to drive anyone spare. Adelphus did everything he could not to work. As a matter of fact, he worked awfully hard at it. And Ulric, who liked to remind them that he had once been a European prince, preferred papers and aetherographic transmission processing. When not required to fight, Ulric actually preferred to fool about with the pack accounts, investments, and correspondences. For his part, Biffy could afford to leave the hat shop in Cyril's capable hands. His head shopkeep might not have the best stylistic eye where millinery was concerned, but the man could sell last week's bread as this week's pudding for three times the price, and make you feel lucky to get it while it was hot. Biffy had watched a young lady wearing dubious amounts of lace walk in looking for gloves and leave carrying three new hats, a fichu, two parasols, and a pair of hair muffs.

So it was that Biffy, Lyall, Rafe, Ulric, and Adelphus

took the first half of the night's watch over the warehouse. He instructed his pack-mates to observe only. Then, right about eight at night, early for most gatherings, people began to arrive. They seemed to represent all walks of laboring life, including full families among their ranks, and were all dressed in Sunday best.

With a start, Biffy realized it was Sunday.

Biffy himself wished he'd dressed down, but he hadn't, which meant he far outclassed everyone there (Sunday best or not). He signaled for Lyall and Rafe to join the modest throng entering the warehouse. They did, lurking to the back and fitting in well enough to pass cursory inspection.

He, Ulric, and Adelphus stayed to the outside, hidden in the shadows, regretting their pretty suits and fine ways.

Professor Lyall had learned over the years never to expect very much. If one didn't cherish high expectations, one was never disappointed and, occasionally, one might even be pleasantly surprised.

Sadly, Lyall would never have called this surprise *pleasant*.

He skulked at the back of the massive room, hidden in plain sight as was his wont. No one noticed him at the best of times – it was his gift. A dubious thing, to be constantly overlooked. After four hundred years, however, he'd learned to appreciate it rather than resent it. *Well, most of the time.*

Rafe, who had a less easy time of skulking, still

managed to lurk with enough subtlety on the other side of the room to pass as human. Rafe was still obviously a predator, large and fierce and deadly. But there were humans like that too, and he'd found a group of them in a corner. Rough, ready, angry men, cracked like leather beneath the weight of the world's use. Standing with them, Rafe could still be one of the things that went bump in the night, just closer to home. The world hid all kinds of monsters – some had too many teeth and some had too much gin.

The gathering rustled in an anticipatory manner, as people murmured and moved about one another. It was much as Lyall expected from a church gathering, except that there were no pews and everyone stood about in a pickling warehouse.

Finally, a man came marching in. Big, confident strides took him up to the small raised platform at the front of the room to the stage that smelled of vinegar. He wore a suit that defied the term, a waistcoat that did no one any favors, least of all him, and a scarf about his neck instead of a cravat. Professor Lyall was the type to make allowances, but *really*. He worried for Biffy's health should the Alpha catch sight of the offending garments.

Lyall wrinkled his nose involuntarily.

The man – he had to assume he was the preacher, nothing less than abject devotion to the almighty could lead anyone to neglect his attire like that – reeked of vinegar, so much so that it brought tears to Lyall's eyes. He wasn't dripping wet, but he clearly bathed in the stuff. *Yech.*

The preacher stood, clapping his hands together, and then began to stride about the small stage, yelling the holy word in a highly aggressive manner. His rhetoric boarded on abusive and was certainly enthusiastic. It was almost theatrical.

He had a big voice and big presence. Not ill formed, possibly even handsome, except that his mouth never stopped moving and his teeth were very... square. His lips were thin, and in speaking, he exposed a great deal of his gums. He was strapping, in a cricket-playing kind of way, with a square jaw – but the noise that emanated from his mouth! It could hardly be called talking. He was brutish towards the English language, harsh with sharp constants and nasal inflections. His vowels were positively abused! Lyall suspected the man's first name was something ridiculously penitent and American like Obadiah or Abner.

The preacher punctuated his sermon with lots of hand gestures and facial grimaces, raising his arms up to heaven, then sweeping them about. He even twirled once or twice and stomped his feet.

"And the Lord came unto you and he said, *you* are the weak and the meek and the prey. And you shall not inherit, oh no! You shall be food for the lords of our holy and true nature. You shall be fodder for the great beasts of the castles. Your children shall be as mere snacks to the supernatural!"

Oh, dear, thought Lyall. *This is not at all what I was expecting. It seems this new cult is quite the opposite of what we feared.*

Instead of preaching the gospel of hating the supernatural set, this man was preaching the gospel of worship. Which, quite frankly, was almost as bad. Thousands of years before Lyall's time, the ancient Egyptians had worshiped werewolves, and everyone knew how badly *that* turned out. The God-Breaker

Plague. Well, maybe not everyone, but everyone that mattered knew.

Still, Lyall was mildly fascinated. The man was a powerful speaker – potent and charismatic. Almost as if he himself had some sort of supernatural ability, drawing all the eyes in the room. A big, commanding presence. A focus point. A tug on the tethers. Riveting and faintly grotesque.

A werewolf Alpha.

That would explain the vinegar smell. If a werewolf wished to disguise his scent, vinegar was a good option. *Even I can't pick up wolf smell through that kind of pong.*

"Make your sacrifices or you too will be called upon to feed the beasts of heaven of your own flesh! Bring forth the next possible candidate!"

An eager (or perhaps nervous) rustle went throughout the room and a young woman was shoved forward. She was dirty and unkempt, her face-paint tear-stained. A lady of the night, no doubt. She clutched to her breast a squalling infant.

Lyall tensed.

"He's a good lad, he is. Never gave me a spot of trouble. Please don't make me—"

"You will burn in the fiery bogs of hell and damnation. Brimstone and soot will rain down upon your head! Steam will scald, and oil will..." yelled the preacher at her. Rather stumbling for good vocabulary, Lyall felt.

The girl trembled.

"Your sacrifice is the only thing that can possibly save you. The beast must be pacified! You think God is kind and merciful? You have not looked into the face of the hellhound at his back!"

The preacher grabbed up the child and set it at his feet. Then he continued to stride around, yelling words at the crowd. Occasionally, he would leap over the child in a kind of wild ritual hopping. This went on for a good half hour, eventually culminating in the man picking up the infant, lifting him high into the air, and the crowd all howling at it.

Lyall exchanged amused glances with Rafe. *Nothing is more droll than humans trying to howl, poor little monkeys.*

No doubt the three others outside were having a good chuckle at the assembled's expense.

Lyall gestured with his head and Rafe followed him out the door in one of those swift dodges only the supernatural could execute unnoticed.

"Did you catch it all, Alpha?" Rafe grinned at Biffy, who was looking poised and quietly diverted by the melodramatics within. The warehouse walls were by no means sufficient to stopper supernatural hearing.

"They're worshiping us." Biffy's tone showed more discomfort than the situation warranted, but it could simply be that he'd caught sight of the preacher's outfit when he first entered.

"It would appear so." Lyall supported the assessment of his Alpha.

Adelphus snorted. "And the infants they keep leaving on our doorstep are what, offerings?"

"Or sacrifices," Lyall shrugged.

"Charming." Ulric curled his lip and turned to pour back into the warehouse, where the congregation still milled and chatted about the excitement of the oratory performance.

Lyall tilted his head. "I think the preacher is himself a

werewolf."

"Hardly possible – he's an American." Adelphus frowned at him.

Lyall quirked a brow. "American werewolves do happen."

"He'll be funny about the head, then, if he is one." Rafe looked thoughtful. "I mean to say, funnier even than what we just heard."

"Most likely." Lyall nodded.

"Well, well, well, how fun is this?" Biffy did not look pleased. "An American werewolf in Greenwich preaching the gospel of supernatural worship and infant-sacrifice. Exactly what I always wanted for Christmas."

Lyall sighed. "It's worse than that, I'm afraid."

"Oh, yes?"

"He smacks of Alpha."

Rafe flinched but agreed. "Didn't get a sniff, but he has that charm, you know? Can't stop looking at him. For all he's got no neckcloth."

Lyall shuddered. "That waistcoat."

"Horrid" – Rafe was morose – "and I don't think he had a shirt on under it. At all." Rafe wasn't particularly fashionable, but this defied all reason.

Biffy gave one of his most winning smiles, almost like one from the bad old days when he was a clever little drone running Lord Akeldama's house and heart. "Oh, well, I can't think of a better reason to fight a man."

"The child-sacrifice thing not bad enough?" Ulric grinned as well.

"We didn't actually kill the infants, even if we were meant to," objected Adelphus. "Don't think *sacrifice* is the right word."

"I think," said Rafe, "we were supposed to eat them."

Adelphus looked properly horrified. "Eat babies? What a preposterous notion. They're almost entirely made of fat, quite detrimental to the digestion. Not to mention the waistline."

Biffy looked approving. "Exactly."

"And they never hold still! So messy." Ulric joined in the spirit of the thing.

"Not to mention the gritty feeling of powdered talc on one's teeth. Yech." Adelphus shuddered.

"Good. Are we agreed, then, no eating babies?" Biffy looked about, and the other four werewolves nodded. "Very good, gentlemen."

Lyall hid his smile. At least the Alpha was using flippancy to disguise his fear over having to actually challenge another werewolf.

While they huddled in conversation in the shadows, the doors to the warehouse creaked open and the congregation began to file out in a mildly cheerful and bubbly mass.

Lyall pushed his Alpha, gently, towards the correct decision. "So, what do we do now?"

"About him?" asked Biffy.

"About him."

Biffy sighed. He removed his hat and twirled it on one hand. "Bah! Confrontation, I suppose. I do hate it so. But going about shirtless with only a waistcoat really cannot be condoned."

"Agreed, Alpha," said Lyall with feeling.

CHAPTER EIGHT

Fight for Your Right to Pulpit

Biffy sighed. Really, this had to be the worst part about being a werewolf. He could tame his hair (which had taken a decade to get right and caused him to invest, rather lucratively, in werewolf-strength pomade called *Parfumé Contrôle du Citron*) and he could tame his temper (which was mild by Alpha standards already, and really didn't take much doing) but he could not tame the way other werewolves behaved – hair or temper. The result was that, in the end, disagreements were settled with claws and teeth. So very undignified.

Biffy was a man of words, not fur. He'd far rather argue, persuade, flatter, or insult an enemy into submission. Fighting simply seemed rather gauche. Still, a man dressed like that pulpit jockey could hardly be expected to obey the social niceties of any society, be it werewolf, English, or even (heaven forfend) American.

Far be it for Biffy not to try civility first, however. Everyone deserved at least one opportunity to run away.

He entered the warehouse, four of his pack at his back. No one made a fuss about them. The werewolves nodded

politely to the remaining supplicants as they passed
through the cavernous space. Hats were tipped to the
ladies. Even Biffy issued all proper courtesies, although
given his superior rank, he wasn't required to be nice.
Still, he was newly minted nobility, and newly moved to
the area – no need to come off as condescending with the
locals.

Even if they were members of a cult.

Even if none of them seemed to know who he was.

Given the meat of the sermon, he supposed, if they
did, they might have run screaming, or cast themselves
at his feet bowing and scraping. Not for the first time,
Biffy was grateful he didn't actually *look* the part of
werewolf. Neither did the others, when all was said and
done.

Lyall looked, most of the time, like a county cleric, or
possibly a banking clerk. Adelphus looked like a mildly
dyspeptic toff, Ulric like a Byronic hero, and Rafe like
the local pub's ferret-legging champion. Of all of them,
Rafe appeared the most wolfish when human, but even
he projected a bashful lumbering that disguised his
predator's grace. Biffy could not have picked a more
unthreatening group from his pack. He was pleased by
this unintended subterfuge.

A few sycophants and disciples remained collected
about the preacher standing on his dais. Some were
requesting private blessings or prayers, others begged for
aid or solace. The squirming child-sacrifice was being
held by a large brutish fellow off to one side. The child's
mother sat crumpled on the floor at the brute's feet,
perhaps having prostrated herself there in an excess of
emotion.

Lacking any other means of modulating the situation,

Biffy fell onto classic societal strictures.

He and his pack waited politely to one side while the man dealt with his flock.

Finally, the preacher turned inquiring eyes upon them.

Biffy inclined his head. "Good evening, sir. My name is Lord Falmouth."

"Welcome! Welcome, gentlemen. I'm Thaddeus Monday."

"Pastor Monday?" Biffy prodded for correct address.

"Yes, sir."

"I'm afraid this is a rather delicate matter."

"I make no allowances for my speech tonight, boys. I come when summoned by the Lord and say the Word as it moves me. Can't say I'm sorry if it disturbed your slumber."

"Oh, no, nothing like that."

"Then has one of your number turned to me and taken up the Following of the Beasts? Because you'll find he has saved himself with righteousness. Nothing you or I can do will turn him back from the bright and snapping path."

"Not that, either." Biffy was mildly amused to see where this was going.

"Well then, well then, you seeking the Word yourselves, young gentlemen? You wish to establish a worship group, perhaps?"

"No, actually. We find your subject matter a smidgen off-putting, to be perfectly honest."

"Hey now, hey now. I thought you Blighty types welcomed werewolves with open arms. That's why I've come. This being the first step in the enlightened direction, I'm merely encouraging the savage truth to out itself."

"You advocate a belief in the superiority of the supernatural?" Biffy wanted verbal evidence to his face.

"Exactly so. Exactly so. Why, I could tell you things that'd raise the hairs on the backs of your necks."

"Could you, indeed?"

"For surely, I could."

"I find I'm well able to do that myself, to be quite frank with you." Biffy edged closer to the man.

How long? How long until the scent – five of them together – finally broke through the vinegar stench surrounding the interloping werewolf loner?

Alpha in my territory.

Biffy moved another step closer.

Carefully, subtly, the others fanned out. Lyall to his right. Adelphus to his left. Rafe towards the brute with the baby. Ulric taking back position, ready to scoop up any leftovers.

They hadn't planned it. They hadn't talked about it. But the pattern fell over them so naturally. Biffy knew well that the others had years together, shaping pack dynamics, but that they netted those years around him with such ease when he was so new to the front of that shape... Biffy glowed with the perfection of it. *My pack.* Tethered strong and sure and at his back. The missing link filled by his Beta brought that last vital element, calm and quiet and there and present. Waiting. All of them waiting, on him. For a movement. For a shift.

Words first.

Biffy leaned in. Closer still. Within striking distance. *Surely, he must smell me now.*

"Lord Falmouth?" The American tensed suddenly. No longer so relaxed. No longer the man in charge. "Not..."

He trailed off. Clearly trying hard to reconcile Biffy's appearance with Biffy's reputation. Or the reputation of werewolves in general – big, rough, and domineering. Or, if not rough, perhaps cruel. Soldiers. Beaters. Brutes. Biffy was none of those things.

A new Alpha for a new Age, Lord Maccon had called him, when Biffy had proved himself to be Alpha. To everyone's surprise. To everyone's continued surprise. *So, I must keep proving myself. Over and over and over again.* Only Lyall had never been surprised. Only Lyall had never wavered in his support. Until he left, of course. *Abandoned me. None of that now.*

Biffy cleared his throat and said, precisely, menacing in tone if not in the deep gruff growl that everyone expected, "I believe you and yours persist in leaving babies on my doorstep. It has become... incommodious."

The man still looked him up and down, disbelieving.

Biffy explained. "While we appreciate the sentiment, we are ill equipped to handle the burden of fatherhood at this time. Perhaps you might assist us in reconnecting the unfortunates with their human relations?"

The man blinked at them. "Who the hell are you? Really? Pranksters? Is it a set-up? A wager? Are you from the Oxford Theologic Society?"

Ulric flinched at such language.

Adelphus huffed at the implication. "Oxford? Really? There's no cause for insult. At least accuse us of being Cambridge men."

"There's a difference?" The preacher sneered.

Utter shock all 'round met that statement.

Ignorant American.

"I beg your pardon!" Biffy straightened and returned his hat to his head in a blatant insult. Such a man did not deserve such a courtesy.

Now I shall have to beat him to a pulp without losing my hat, on principle.

A delicate cough and Lyall slid forward slightly. Yes, well, perhaps the time had come for Biffy to hold his tongue and stick his nose in the air in silent autocratic judgment. Which he did.

"Professor Lyall." Lyall introduced himself and stuck out his hand in a friendly American manner. "Good evening, Mr Monday. I'm afraid we may be at a bit of an impasse. You see, you appear to be a lone werewolf. It is against protocol for one such as yourself to be within pack territory without calling upon us first. Regardless of the rabble-rousing talk, and the baby-depositing action, we must rectify your presence here with werewolf requirements. We would like this matter settled so we may return to the peace of our normal pursuits. We are recently moved to this neighborhood and were under the initial impression that Greenwich was cult-free. Now, the normal way of these things provides two possible solutions..."

The American crossed his arms and smiled that big gum-ridden smile. "Oh, now, boys, I think I may know where this is going. You think I ain't prepared for this? You think I ain't heard how things went down here in London a few months ago? Young Alpha, untried, untested, and weak, yet holding the most prestigious pack in Britain?"

Biffy rolled his eyes. Wonderful. *Why does everyone think I'm weak?* He took out his handkerchief and waved it at Lyall in a *here we go again* kind of manner.

Hard to tell with his beloved Beta, but it looked like the professor was trying to hide a smile.

Lyall cleared his throat. "As I was saying. Traditionally, you would leave, now, quietly and untroubled. And I would leave England entirely, if I were you – the Crown frowns upon talk of supernatural supremacy. You'll be registered as a malcontent, of course. As will your, ahem, followers."

"And my other options, little man?"

Lyall gave a tiny smile. "You've only the one. You fight."

"You?"

Lyall examined his nails. "If you like."

"But you're not the Alpha."

"Certainly not."

"Well, that seems pointless."

Biffy sighed. "Professor, if you would?"

Lyall moved to him quickly, assisting in the removal of his coat, waistcoat, and cravat. Biffy hated this part. It never got less embarrassing, stripping in public. But he refused to destroy a perfectly nice suit. Even if it wasn't one of his favorites.

He toed off his shoes and dropped his trousers. Which left him in only his shirt and hat. He'd long since given over undergarments. He didn't need them for warmth, and they complicated matters.

Lyall gathered the garments delicately and placed them on the dais. Leaving his own hands unencumbered, just in case he needed to shift himself.

Biffy appreciated the backup. The man before him was bigger than he was, angrier than he was, and likely more vicious. But then again, most other Alpha wolves were. Frankly, most other werewolves were bigger, angrier, and more vicious, Alpha or otherwise. Lyall was the only wolf Biffy had ever met who matched him in size and temperament.

The American was laughing. "You? You dandy boy? You want to fight me? Is this a joke?"

Biffy sighed. "Not that I object to the destruction of your current garments, but will you be shifting without removing your coat first? It can inhibit movement. Wouldn't want to put you at a disadvantage." Biffy paused, his lip gently curled. "More of a disadvantage than you already are."

The man looked around. No one else was laughing. His remaining followers were standing back, puzzled. The four other werewolves in the room remained calm and quiet and watchful.

Were this an official challenge for supremacy, they could not interfere, merely enforce the circle. But, so far, the challenge had not been properly issued. So, they could step in, if they liked.

Biffy didn't want them at risk, so he would have to force the point. "Shall we try this again, Mr Monday? I am Lord Falmouth, Alpha of the London Pack. Do you wish to challenge my leadership, as you are a loner in my territory?" The formality of the words warmed him, even as their crassness bit his human nature. All too often, Biffy wished that wolves might be a little less direct.

The man stopped laughing. "What is this cussed foolishness? I don't want to have to kill you, boy. You need only bow before me. Challenge has already been issued. What'd you think the children were, offerings? Come at me."

No one moved.

"Wait" – that was Ulric – "You sent infants as preemptive weregild in lieu of challenge blood?"

Lyall seemed to follow this line of thinking. He gave

a small cough. "In this day and age, Mr Monday, we do not even require a dead rabbit. A simple inscription in blood on the back of a calling card would suffice."

Biffy did not like to be confused. He knew the protocols for challenge. They'd been impressed upon him from the moment he proved himself to be an Alpha with pack intentions. Challenge could be issued many ways, usually with words written in blood, occasionally with the slap of a bloodied glove in the old-fashioned dueling manner. Years ago, it was the slaying of a deer in contested territory. Live babies seemed a bit excessive.

The man shrugged. "Cultural differences. So, you accept my challenge then, boy?"

Biffy knew he was not very prepossessing, standing there in his shirt, top hat, and nothing else. But he was still Alpha – dignity was paramount.

He nodded. "I accept."

Lyall sighed. *Why must it always come to this?* His Biffy hated to fight. He'd always hated to fight. Although he had been a spectacular fencer before he turned wolf, it had been more a form of dance than a battle of steel.

Yet a challenge had been issued and must be accepted. The Alpha was present and in fighting form. Lyall could not fight for him. Would not. It was for Biffy to do this now.

He glanced at the other pack members. None of them seemed particularly tense or upset. Biffy might not have much confidence in himself, but he had his pack's support. *I wonder if he knows that.*

Then Biffy changed shape. And Lyall realized that

while twenty years might not be very long in werewolf time, it was long enough for some things to change a great deal.

His young Alpha had already mastered the shift. His beautiful Alpha. Smooth and easy with barely a hint of pain. Where once Biffy had fought it so hard and so fiercely, it seemed he had now accepted shape change with that same fierceness. Almost as if he welcomed the pain.

He was fast with it, too. Fully formed wolf long before the American had even started to follow him into the beast.

Biffy's fine white shirt ripped easily around his now wolf body to fall beneath him. He'd grown into his fur, too. Still lean and muscled and svelte, not bulky, but his wolf looked comfortable, rich chocolate with an oxblood ruff and stomach. His eyes were fierce and sharp and yellow as buttercups.

The challenger, however, got all caught up in his coat and trousers, shifting without stripping first. He had to fight himself free in a hugely undignified manner. The end result being that his waistcoat survived entirely intact and still on his body, even though that body was now a wolf. It was beyond absurd-looking. And such an ugly waistcoat! Striped, like that of a footman.

This had the werewolves all about chuckling quietly into their cuffs. Except Lyall, whose attention wasn't on the challenger or his waistcoat.

He watched Biffy's stillness and calm. His contained power. Biffy's Alpha nature was flowing from him now, fully formed and cloaking him in power. Nothing was visible, it appeared almost more like an odorless, pulsing smell. *Obey. Obey. Obey.*

Alpha nature was more obvious when Biffy was a wolf, and more obvious to Lyall, who knew to look for it. Lyall saw it in the flash of buttercup eyes, careful and contained and calculating.

Fighting smart. So few wolves could do that.

The challenger certainly couldn't. He howled as he shifted, turning beast in the worst way, slow horror and monstrous suffering. He wasn't happy with what he was, had never fully accepted it, for all he tried to glorify it from the pulpit.

Once fully shifted, panting slightly from residual pain, the challenger charged, teeth bared and drooling slightly. He looked like a creature from the Dark Ages. No intelligence was there, only instinct and rage.

Biffy moved almost imperceptibly, a flicker of muscles, and he was on the other side of the dais, still sitting, still calm. Still, miraculously, wearing his top hat.

The American wolf flew past where Biffy had just been, and barreled off the stage, stumbling over the edge.

He fell close to where Rafe stood.

Lyall flicked Rafe a look and a nod. Rafe backed up a tiny bit, lip curled.

The challenger was already up and around and charging Biffy again. But he had come too close to the circle's edge, and he did not seem to know proper protocols at all. They shouldn't be surprised. After all, he had sent babies as weregild.

Rafe began stripping down. None of Biffy's reticence, nor did he need Lyall's assistance (he was in his layman's clothing). His shape shift was long and uncomfortable to watch. Rafe was relatively young and not an Alpha. Lyall did not watch, refocusing on the fight before him. He trusted his pack-mate to be ready. Rafe would act on instinct. He would maintain the circle with tooth and claw. He would follow the strongest Alpha without question. Whoever that ended up being.

Biffy dodged another charge, only this time he stuck out a paw, almost casually, scraping away the challenger's flesh from ear to shoulder, pulling deep red gashes up through dirty brown fur.

Now was the time when the American should fold, falling over to his back and exposing his belly in supplication. First blood and a clearly superior opponent in power, position, brains, and speed. But he did not. The gash only seemed to enrage him further.

Lyall frowned. Perhaps this was even more abnormal than he had already thought. Perhaps this challenger was not simply a loner but too long a loner. To long without pack. Or too old being both Alpha and loner. Perhaps he was mad under Alpha's curse.

Sending babies as challenge offerings certainly didn't smack of sanity.

Well – Lyall was philosophical – *at least he didn't send us dead babies.*

Customarily, pack challenges did not end in death. It was considered a waste of supernatural life. Although there were always exceptions. Sometimes, challenges were issued by wolves who wished to die, who had lived too long and were ready to leave in blood and glory – an honorable end in an Alpha's jaw. Lyall hoped for that himself someday. Not yet, of course. He wasn't done yet.

Lyall twitched in uncertainty. This fight was not clean. Or it was from Biffy's perspective, but not from Mr Monday's.

The man was unhinged. He kept simply charging, no leaps, no twists, no swipes, nothing to indicate technique, or interest in a proper battle.

So, Biffy kept dodging and swiping. The challenger was now bleeding from multiple lacerations. The slow black blood of immortality oozed down onto the stage, making him slip.

Biffy lost his hat in the scuffle.

Lyall retrieved it for him.

End it, Lyall tried to think at him. This long, drawn-out suffering was no kind of proper fight.

Biffy seemed to understand, for in a rush, he twisted his dodge and went in for the other wolf's neck. He dove under, and with a firm, full bash of his forehead, Biffy upended the heavier wolf and threw him to his side.

Biffy avoided the challenger's scrabbling claws with ease and in one smooth move clamped his jaws fully around the other wolf's neck. Lord Maccon had taught his protégé well. Lyall knew without a doubt that Biffy's canines pressed upon Monday's windpipe. He would apply a steady pressure until things ended, one way or another.

Lyall could not have been prouder. This was a perfect subjugation move, beautifully executed, elegant and final without being deadly.

Ulric and Adelphus clapped. It was, after all, very prettily done.

But the other wolf would not be still. He writhed even as his air flow was restricted, even as Biffy's other teeth cut in closer and closer to the main artery of his neck.

Lyall shook his head, sorrowed. Either Monday did not know the proper form at all, or he was too far gone in madness to care.

"Submit, you fool!" said Adelphus, but the wolf was beyond human speech.

Biffy's eyes, harsh and yellow, looked over at them from around his struggling mouthful. The buttercup color was filled with sadness.

Lyall met them in compassion and understanding. He inclined his head, not that Biffy needed his permission. But he thought it might help, in the end, if it was given.

The yellow eyes closed, once. Then Biffy lifted his head high, at the same time biting down as hard as he could and twisting aside. He slammed the other wolf's head to the floor, breaking his neck, constricting his air, and severing the main blood flow to his brain all at the same time.

Even supernatural creatures can die.

Biffy let go as soon as his enemy's body stopped twitching. The burnt iron of old blood filled his mouth, foul and flawed and tainted. This was nothing like the fresh kill of a wild creature, coppery and sweet. Immortals never tasted good – there was no freshness left in them to enjoy.

He sat back and tried not to shake himself like a wet dog, or sneeze.

Ulric stripped the waistcoat off of the dead wolf. It seemed almost insultingly undignified to leave it on him. Fortunately, it had been ruined in the scuffle. Just to be safe, and because he was twitchy with having had to kill, Biffy savaged the hideous thing into tiny pieces. It cleaned his mouth of some of the blood, too.

Those supplicants still present and not fallen into shocked stupors gasped in titillated horror. Funny how the taking of a life had held them silently in thrall, but the destruction of a vest gave them license to react.

Biffy could hear them gossiping down at the pub the next day. *First, the new Alpha killed the visiting American, and then, well then, he destroyed the man's waistcoat!*

The ensuing silence eventually yielded up hysterics on the part of some of the congregation, a roar of anger from the brute with the child, and general discombobulation from everyone else present. Well, Greenwich wasn't accustomed to such carryings-on.

The pack sprang into action.

Adelphus removed the child from the brute and disposed of both. The child back to the mother, the brute to the floor in a crumpled heap. Not dead, just momentarily incapacitated with a well-aimed fist.

Ulric explained in his most arrogant and commanding tone that the others would have to clean up the mess and bury the body. Since it wasn't the winner's responsibility, and the challenger hadn't brought a second, there was no one else to do the deed. They should have thought of that before they started listening, willy-nilly, to pedantic Americans.

Biffy and Rafe remained in wolf form. No sense in adding nudity into the mix at this juncture. Might cause a riot.

Lyall suggested that word be spread about the neighborhood concerning the unfortunate demise of the nascent cult leader, and that perhaps they might consider congregating again tomorrow night? The proper local pack would come down and instruct them in niceties of wolf-worship. (Of course, they had absolutely no intention of continuing the farce of supernatural supremacy, but it wouldn't do to disencumber the supplicants of their leader and their rhetoric all at once.) Besides, the pack still needed to return the children.

"We should bring the wassail with us," Lyall said to Adelphus.

"Good idea."

They returned to the pack house at least pleased to have solved the mystery, if a little perturbed to see it end in such an unsportsmanlike manner. It was always disappointing when a challenge ended in death.

Biffy went up to his room to change and did not come back down. He didn't feel up to more pack histrionics right away. Adelphus and Ulric could handle explaining and gossip and such as the others returned home.

Biffy moped. It wasn't gentlemanly, but it was the truth. And his tummy was a mite queasy. Fortunately, no one witnessed his weakness.

Although it seemed Lyall guessed, because he sent Rumpet up with tea.

Shortly thereafter, the Beta himself followed, accompanied by consolatory biscuits. "My lord, may I come in?"

Somehow, Biffy didn't mind his Beta. Lyall's presence was more a soothing balm than an imposition, even when Biffy wished to be alone. It was probably a Beta characteristic, or simply because he was Professor Randolph Lyall and always easy to be around for everyone.

Biffy had not bothered to dress again. Instead, he was wearing his favorite quilted velvet dressing gown. It was a very fine rich blue, lined in satin. He felt almost royal in it.

He gestured for Lyall and the biscuits to enter.

CHAPTER NINE

Tethered and Forgotten

Lyall set down his offering of shortbread and stood, looking down on Biffy. The blue dressing gown was quite fetching. *This Alpha – my Alpha – has excellent taste. At least I need not worry on that score anymore.*

Does he want to be left alone? Lyall hadn't yet fully matched to his new Alpha's moods.

He'd known Biffy before metamorphosis, young and bright and free of cares except for the wishes of his vampire master. At that time, Lyall could have predicted drone Biffy's wants. His curious bright interest in the world and its machinations. He'd wanted very little then.

He'd known Biffy directly after, newly metamorphosed, struggling to learn to become what he'd never wanted, to accept his new afterlife. At that time too, Lyall could have anticipated werewolf Biffy's needs. Sometimes, he had. Sometimes, anticipation, need, and want had all been the same thing.

But he didn't know Alpha Biffy – this mature hunter with a pack at his back. So sure of his wolf and yet not of his command. In control, but only when he was not paying attention, questioning himself the rest of the time. So comfortable in his fur and fighting, and yet shifting and twitchy in a beautiful blue dressing gown after dealing out death.

Lyall saw nothing for it but the direct approach. One that Biffy, no doubt, still loathed, but which Lyall had come to understand had its place in werewolf dynamics, if not in polite society.

"Do you wish to talk about it, Alpha?" From what Lyall knew of Biffy before surviving the bite, killing of this kind was outside his purview. He wasn't a soldier and had never trained as one, even after becoming werewolf. He'd served his civic duty to the Crown as a newly minted pup in the Home Office, practicing espionage, not in the front lines, not even in the shadows as an assassin.

Biffy sipped his tea. "Blood is so messy. And the iron taste of immortality is never pleasant."

"No," agreed Lyall. "No, it's not, is it?"

Biffy nodded for Lyall to sit.

Lyall settled near enough to be a reassurance and a comfort, but not so close as to be thought intruding – any more than he already was.

Biffy looked into his tea for a long moment, as if there, in the leaf, were all the answers.

"Lyall, would you tell me something of pack protocol, without taking insult? I am afraid the question may be indelicate."

Lyall hid his surprise with consummate skill and hedged his answer. "I'm no howler, so I may not know the answer you seek. I could summon one to visit us, if it were a matter of origin and specifics."

"But you are old enough to know most of the right

way of things."

"Yes. I'm old enough." Lyall didn't know why, but he held his breath.

Biffy winced, looking away from tea and into fire. His blue eyes were tinted yellow by the shifting flames – a hint at the wolf within. "Is it wrong, what we did, you and I, before you left?"

Of all the things to be asked. "By whose standards?"

Biffy gave a humorless smile. "Oh, I do not mean morally or socially. I know what *they* think. I mean by pack protocols. Are like-minded gentleman werewolves not supposed to share intimacy?" He chose his words with exacting care.

Lyall tried not to flinch or blush, keeping his breathing slow and relaxed. He tried not to be excited by this line of inquiry. He tried not to want the reasons behind it. "Nothing carnal is held sacred that I know of. It's not common, but it's not forbidden, either. Werewolves, like vampires, have always been less bound by the limits humans will pose on their own desires. Within reason, of course. Both parties should be agreeable and willing, and capable of undertaking an informed decision. I always felt we were all such things, back then."

"Yes." Biffy smiled at him. "And perhaps more."

Lyall nodded. On his part, certainly more. "Yes."

"So, now that I am your Alpha in truth? Now it is forbidden? It would be considered taking advantage of my position, perhaps?"

Lyall blinked, startled. Why would he think that? Alpha was a feeling, a necessity, a control, not exactly a position of authority so much as a state of existence. There was no abuse to the power, not in a good Alpha.

And Biffy was a good one, for all he questioned himself.

Is this what I have wrought? This doubt in him? When I returned with all my need not to push, not to impose, not to rely upon what we once had? Was I damaging him? Biffy clearly required some form of reassurance. So, like any good Beta, Lyall sacrificed his own pride for that of his Alpha.

"No. Oh, no. I thought you would not want me back like that. I thought that I was comfort then, nothing more."

Biffy flinched and looked, at last, at him. "I let you leave, thinking so little of us? Thinking that?"

"I left thinking that. My choice. You had so much ahead of you, so much to learn. So much changing. I thought twenty years was a long time, and it would be easy if I returned to you without expectations."

Biffy turned towards Lyall fully, angling his body, reaching out with his fine, strong hands. He trailed three fingers down the side of Lyall's cheek, as if learning the feel of the soft beard that hadn't been there before. "It was more than comfort."

Biffy smelled of sandalwood and Bond Street pomade, and a little of blood and battle and the forests that had once, eons ago, lined the banks of the Thames. Wolf and man, wild and civilized in equal measure. He smelled of home, and safety, and guidance, and need.

My Alpha. Mine.

Lyall nodded, and opened himself to his Alpha. To his lover. "It was more than comfort for me as well."

Biffy let the words be enough. Coating him with joy and

gratitude.

Then Lyall slid in against him – quiet and warm and present. This part was so achingly familiar, it almost hurt him to allow it in again. Even though he'd been waiting so long with only the thought of this moment to hope for.

"Twenty years, Lyall." He said it on an exhale, not so much accusation as plea.

"I told you it would take time."

"Twenty years!" He knew Lyall would sense the question in the accusation.

But it was not in his Beta's nature to be confrontational. "Lady Kingair is a great responsibility for a Beta. She took much of my attention. Plus, there was a war to fight."

Biffy plucked at a loose thread in the divan. "I wouldn't have thought her your type."

"I don't know. I've always liked my women a little gruff and brash, and my men suave and broken."

Biffy winced. "And did you and she—?"

"No. Never."

Biffy really wanted to ask for further details and really didn't want to ask. Twenty years was a long time for a werewolf to be celibate. They were noted for a healthy appetite in all things. Surely, there must have been someone. A small voice reminded Biffy that he himself hadn't partaken. Which was embarrassing, in its way.

Well, he said to himself, trying to justify decades of celibacy, *I had a lot to do. I had to become an Alpha. I had to... Excuses. I had to wait. I wanted to wait.* But Lyall didn't need to know that. And Biffy didn't want to know if Lyall had also waited. Because he wasn't sure which would be worse – that he had or that he had not.

Saying nothing wasn't correct either. "There's been

no one for me."

Against him, Lyall went perfectly still.

Biffy soldiered on. "I had to learn a great deal. To be a werewolf. An Alpha. To lead pack. To cry challenge and to win."

"No one? For twenty years?"

"I had to heal too, from loss."

Lyall nodded. "Your family. Lord Akeldama. The other immortality that you gave up for this one."

"Yes, that too."

"Too?"

"Twenty years. I have waited long enough."

"For me?" Such a wealth of confusion in Lyall's voice. Of lack of value.

Biffy felt the pain in the question as if it were a pressure at the base of his throat, stoppering breath. *Oh, no. I never thought. I never considered that he would not think himself worthy. Of course.* Lyall would never think to put himself on the list of loves lost. Would never think of himself as second, or third, or fourth in Biffy's affections. He was Beta, born to live his life for others.

"Silly man. The main loss I had to cope with was yours." There. Lyall could make of that what he would. That Biffy missed him for his gentle care as Beta werewolf, or that Biffy missed him as man, and friend, and lover.

Hesitantly, Biffy set his hands on Lyall's shoulders. Careful not to upset the line of the jacket. Careful because he wished to grab so badly.

Then Lyall tilted his head slightly. That birdlike movement that said he was considering carefully what he would say next.

Biffy decided to stop being careful. He pulled Lyall

against him and held him as tightly as he could, hands stroking down that familiar back, curling up to the back of his neck, messing up that perfectly styled hair, so much longer now with the aftereffects of mortality.

Lyall sighed and relaxed against him. Lyall, who never relaxed. He pressed his nose against Biffy's neck, nuzzling under the collar of the robe, breathing him in.

"You smell like home." Lyall murmured it into Biffy's throat.

"While you, on the other hand, still wear the scent of desert sands about you. Foreign and not right. Come to bed? We can work on fixing that condition." Biffy expected resistance. It was the middle of the night. There were things still to do. The pack was awake. And Lyall was refined and reserved, never wild or uncontrolled. So, most of the time, was Biffy.

"Will we be done in time for supper?" was Lyall's only token resistance.

"Of course. What do you take me for, some kind of monster?" But Biffy's hands were now fisted in Lyall's jacket and he was almost dragging him towards the bed.

For two extremely cultivated men, reunions, it turned out, could be a messy business. Rushed, and fumbling, and sloppy, and desperate, but also sweet and wondering. Twenty years *was* a long time, and Biffy wanted to relearn every inch of his lover's body.

He remembered, of course, what those perfectly tailored nondescript suits covered. His Lyall was all lean muscle and smooth skin. There was a little cluster of freckles on his right shoulder blade that needed to be checked and licked – still there. *Good.* There was the way the hair on his head tapered down to a *V* at the base of his neck, that needed to be checked and nibbled – still there, still elicited the same whimper of pleasure. *Good.*

Lyall was doing the same. They hadn't had much time together before he left with the Kingair Pack, but they'd made good use of it. There was a lot to remind each other of. The same taste, different smells, same kisses, different touches, the best kind of reminding. Even while it was hurried and desperate, it was also perfectly rapturous.

There was something more there too, something in the strands of tether between Alpha and Beta, as if they were knitting together the last pieces of their souls.

When they lay tangled and supine, satiated and sticky, Biffy asked about it. "Did you feel that?"

Lyall understood, of course. "A resettling of the tethers, yours and mine."

"Is it normal?"

"What is normal?"

Biffy glared at him.

Lyall pressed Biffy's nose with his finger in the manner of a playful adult to a frustrated child.

"Randolph!" Biffy resorted to Lyall's given name, which he knew they both hated.

"I only know what I have felt before. Previously, when I have settled into a new Alpha, it usually comes along gradually. But then, I never slept with any of them so early on in our relationship. And never willingly."

Biffy flinched from that. He knew Lyall had been abused by Lord Vulkasin when that Alpha had succumbed to the curse. Insanity was the greatest of werewolf horrors, and Biffy dreaded that fate. Although he was young and he likely had hundreds of years, he still flinched away from the horror of his future. He did not deserve sympathy for what would be, when Lyall had once dealt with it personally, every day.

"I will go to the God-Breaker Plague before I let myself get that far gone. I swear it," Biffy vowed.

Lyall stroked Biffy's hair, placid and reassuring. "Hush, now. I've got you. Can you feel how strong it is?"

"Yes, that's why I was asking about it. I mean to say, I can feel my tethers to the rest of the pack, but it's not like this."

"It's different. Thicker, tighter. I feel possessive in a way I had not before," Lyall agreed, but did not seem upset.

"Sex complicates matters." Biffy puffed out his checks, afraid.

Lyall nudged him. "Sometimes, it simplifies them. It brings them here, to this place, to need and gratification and connection. I am entirely yours now."

Biffy buried his face in Lyall's neck and inhaled. "Yes, you are."

"And you are mine."

The Alpha in Biffy balked at the statement, but also liked it. He tested the tether between them, a small emotional tug. It wasn't a chain or a leash. It wasn't binding. He didn't think it would become so. It simply was.

Lyall hummed and tugged gently back.

Biffy started at the feeling and glared at him.

"When you're as old as I am, you think there are no more firsts." Lyall was actually grinning. His forgettable face made memorable and beautiful by discovery.

"Are you complaining?" Biffy teased, with an edge of worry. He liked being a first for a werewolf hundreds of years old. But this was so very sudden and unmoving in its intensity.

"Certainly not. It feels right. It is odd, but I feel as if I am anchoring you. As if this is what a Beta is meant to be, and before I was merely acting the part as best I could. This is somehow more real."

Biffy kissed him for his candor, and because, even now, he couldn't stop touching him.

"Four hundred years to find my place." Lyall folded against him, resting his cheek in the divot beneath Biffy's shoulder.

Biffy shifted to get more comfortable, winding his legs through his lover's, pressing Lyall close with long strokes and firm hands. "I guess the fact that I had to wait for twenty is not so bad, by comparison."

Biffy felt that he had given everything. And taken everything. They were what they were, and the world would have to accept it.

Lyall was heavy against him, dozing off. Biffy thought he was asleep until he spoke. It was so quiet, Biffy almost missed his words, even with supernatural hearing.

"We will have a long time now, you and I. Together. Must be, with a tether this strong. I think I can hold you here, hold you back."

"From what, my love?"

"From Alpha's curse. From madness."

Biffy choked and nodded, but did not stop his petting, did not relax his hold.

Soon enough, Lyall slept against him.

Biffy wept silently into sandy hair – overcome with relief and lost loneliness and the possibility of forever.

EPILOGUE

In a Neat Little Bow, With Squash

The next evening, in the hostile territory of the warehouse, the entire London Pack assembled behind their Alpha in protective battle formation, consolidated and supportive. After a round of crossed arms and intimidating glares, which humbled the assembled cult members into fearful murmurs, Biffy redistributed the babies back to their respective parents.

There had been some debate on the efficacy of this. Would the infants not, next thing, turn up on some vampire's doorstep? Lyall argued that the warped preacher had used Alpha abilities of persuasion and coercion, and with him gone, the children were much less at risk. However, even he was concerned about lingering influences.

So, Biffy made (what he hoped was) a very eloquent speech on the indigestibility of human infants. It took a great deal of persuading to get the congregation to accept that child sacrifice was not something werewolves particularly desired on a regular basis. Biffy had to draw metaphors of a rather visceral nature, and extol the virtues of big game and the inferiority of fat baby pudge.

He found that it was easier to convince the followers that werewolves could be deluded by fake sacrifices of not-babies (like ancient Greek gods) than outright persuade them wolves didn't want the babies at all. Accordingly, Biffy organized a demonstration.

Adelphus marched in, carrying a large squash dressed in swaddling clothes. Channing made a special appearance already in wolf form (so he couldn't say anything and mess the plan up, and because he made for their most impressive wolf). The massive white wolf jumped on the swaddled squash, savaged it into submission, and then dashed off (late for an appointment with his haberdasher).

This seemed to convince everyone, and offerings of squashes, in various states of dress and undress, began appearing on the new house's doorstep. The clavigers got quickly sick of the vegetable, and they began donating them to the workhouse. Everyone was happy. Except maybe the squash.

Robin, as it turned out, was a foundling with no family to speak of. After much begging and pleading, Biffy decided it was odd but acceptable if the pack wished to adopt him. Hemming was delighted. The government was skeptical but willing. Mrs Whybrew and her daughter were permanently installed in the nursery, and life settled, as much as it might, with two infants in residence.

Biffy changed the curtains from purple to royal blue.

Lyall moved his few belongings into Biffy's quarters. The pack was carefully neutral about this relocation. Although Lyall caught Rafe and Hemming giggling in a suspicious manner the first time he emerged from Biffy's quarters of an evening.

Only Channing said anything, because Channing was never one to hold his tongue when insult could be proffered. He quirked a brow at them across the breakfast table a few nights into the new arrangement. "If this is a new pack hierarchy bonding policy, I hope you don't expect me to join in the fun."

"No one ever expects you to join in, Channing," replied Lyall.

Biffy smiled. "You'd spoil our fun."

Channing nodded. "Good." He stood and went to retrieve his hat and coat. Then stuck his head back in before he left. "About bloody time."

Lyall ducked his head, then looked up at his Alpha through his lashes.

Biffy ate a piece of pork pie and gloried in the fact that, while Lyall might be embarrassed, his sandy eyes were no longer sad.

And now, here is a special print edition *only* bonus short story: *The Curious Case of the Werewolf That Wasn't*.

What follows is a short tale of mummies, werewolves, and well-preserved felines set in the Parasolverse. Alessandro Tarabotti and his valet, Floote, are on a mission in Egypt when they encounter visiting tourists and things go pie shaped.

A Note on Chronology

This story is set in the 1840s. It is thus about 30 years before the Parasol Protectorate series and about 55 years before the novella you just finished, *Romancing the Werewolf.*

THE

CURIOUS CASE OF THE WEREWOLF THAT WASN'T

(TO SAY NOTHING OF THE
MUMMY THAT WAS AND THE
CAT IN THE JAR)

GAIL CARRIGER

GAIL CARRIGER LLC

THE CURIOUS CASE OF THE WEREWOLF THAT WASN'T

(To Say Nothing of the Mummy that Was and the Cat in the Jar)

Egypt 1841

"Yoo-hoo!"

Alessandro Tarabotti's forehead crinkled under his grey top hat. Was that some peculiar birdsong?

"Yoo-hoo, Sandy!" No, it was a voice hallooing at him across the broiling humanity of the bazaar.

Mr Tarabotti was so thoroughly distracted upon hearing such a name hollered at him in such a place and voice, that he relaxed his grip. The place was Luxor. The voice was just the kind that bled the inner ear, trumpeting out a nasal ode to abundant schooling and little attention towards the details of it. His loosened grip allowed the scrubby native boy with terrified fly-ridden eyes to rip himself away and scuttle down a convenient alleyway, vanishing round a pile of broken pottery.

"Well, that's torn it." Alessandro threw the scrap of material he was left holding onto the dirt street. He squinted into the alley, eyes adjusting slowly to the slatted light that crept through reed mats stretched far above. High houses and narrow streets – who would have thought Egypt a place of shadows and shade?

"Sandy, old chap!" The voice was getting closer.

"Who knows you here, sir?" asked Floote.

"More to the point, who would dare yoo-hoo at me?" Mr Tarabotti turned from the empty alleyway to glare at his valet as though the greeting were somehow Floote's fault.

Floote pivoted and gestured softly with his right hand. His left was occupied in holding onto a large glass specimen jar.

The yoo-hooer hove into sight. Alessandro winced. The man wore the most remarkably bright blue frock coat, double breasted, with brass buttons up the front. He sported a pair of Rumnook's stained-glass binocular spectacles perched atop his tiny nose, and a limp cravat. In Mr Tarabotti's world, nothing excused a limp cravat, even the dead heat of Egypt at high noon.

"Do I know that repulsive-looking blighter?"

Floote twisted his mouth slightly to one side.

"Quite right, quite right. Someone from my early days. Before I cultivated a brain. School, perhaps?" Mr Tarabotti awaited his fate, brushing a nonexistent speck of dust from the sleeve of his own gold frock coat. Single breasted, mind you, with pearl buttons and a deceptively simple cut.

"Blasted English, blemishing about the world. Is nowhere safe?"

Floote, who was himself an Englishman, did not point

out that Alessandro Tarabotti, of a similarly unfortunate over-education as the man approaching, dressed and spoke like an Englishman. He didn't actually look like one, of course, boasting a long line of ancestors who had invested heavily in being dark, hook-nosed, and brooding.

Mr Tarabotti continued grousing, right up until the yoo-hooer was within earshot. "I mean to say, Floote my man, what are your countrymen about these days? You'd think they'd leave at least one small corner of the planet to the rest of us. But no, here they are, shiny as all get up, ever expanding the Empire."

"We have benefited considerably from integration of the supernatural."

"Well, it's hell on the rest of us. Do stop it, will you?"

"Very good, sir."

"Yoo-hoo, yoo-hoo!" The man came to a wheezing halt before them, sounding like an exhausted steam engine, and trailing some species of suitable young lady in his corpulent wake. "Sandy Dandy the Italian? By Jove, it is you! Fancy, fancy, fancy!"

Alessandro, who did not like the name Sandy Dandy the Italian, lifted his monocle and examined the man downwards through it.

The man said, to the monocle, "Baronet Percival Phinkerlington. How d'you do?"

At least he had the good grace to introduce himself. Mr Tarabotti put down his eyepiece pointedly. Really, what a thing to do to one's cravat.

"You knew my brother, I believe."

The face above the unfortunate neck cloth did have a familiar something about the eyes and mouth. "Good Lord, old Pink's kid brother?"

The man grinned and doffed his top hat. "Right you are! Fancy I was a bit smaller back when you knew me last!"

"Practically half the man you are now."

"You remember our sister?"

The lady in question went red under Mr Tarabotti's indifferent glance. He didn't bother with the monocle. She bobbed a trembling curtsy. Ladies always caught the blush-and-flutters upon meeting Alessandro Tarabotti.

He bowed. "Miss Phinkerlington."

"Leticia, you remember Sandy? Mr Tarabotti, I should say. Italian chappie, went to Oxford with Eustace. Used to bowl for New College. Toddled down for a stopover one session break. The same time father had himself that whole werewolf pack visiting." He turned back to Mr Tarabotti. "Fancy meeting you here. In Egypt of all places!"

"Indeed." Alessandro tried to remember why he would bother visiting this man's family. Had it been an assignment? Investigating the werewolves? Or had he been there to kill someone? Perhaps just a mild maiming?

Sir Percival leaned in conspiratorially. "You ought to see to your man there, Sandy. You realize he's got his arm 'round a jam jar of dead cat?"

"Mmm, yes, preserved in some of my best formaldehyde."

The baronet gave a nervous laugh. "Always were a bit peculiar, Sandy. Eustace seemed to like you well enough. I say, this may be Egypt, but trailing about with dead cats – not the done thing."

"I have an eccentric aunt," replied Mr Tarabotti, as though that were explanation enough.

"Don't we all, my dear fellow? Don't we all?"

"It's her cat. Or it was her cat, I should say."

Miss Phinkerlington noticed the valet with the glass jar full of cat for the first time. She coloured a sandy sage and turned away, pretending interest in the bustling natives ebbing and flowing around them. A proper Englishwoman must find it a spectacle indeed, that tide of humanity in its multicoloured robes, veiled or turbaned according to sex, loud and malodorous regardless.

"Floote." Alessandro used Miss Phinkerlington's discomfort as an excuse. "Shove off, will you? Find out what happened to our young friend. I'll see you back at the hotel."

Floote nodded and disappeared across the bazaar, cat in hand.

Sir Percival seemed to take that as an end to the business. "Well, well, well, what a thing to see you here. Been a while, old chap. Came for the climate, myself. Wettest winter in a donkey's years, decided on a bit of a change. Thought Egypt might suit."

"Imagine England having a wet winter. Remarkable."

"Yes, yes, well, Egypt, here, a bit, eh, warmer, you understand, than I was expecting. But we've been taking the aether regular-like. Haven't we, Leticia? Keeps a body cool." The baronet jerked his head up at the three large balloons hovering high above Luxor. They were tethered by long cords to a landing platform dockside. Well, that explained the man's abysmal choice in eyewear. Tinted spectacles were recommended for high floating.

The baronet persisted in his social niceties. "And are you having an agreeable trip?"

"Can't stand travel," replied Mr Tarabotti. "Bad for the digestion and ruins one's clothes."

"Too true." The baronet looked suitably sombre. "Too true." Moving hurriedly on from a clearly distasteful topic, he asked, "Staying at Chumley's Inn, are you, Sandy?"

Alessandro nodded. It was the only place to stay in Luxor. Alexandria and Cairo provided a number of respectable hotels, but Luxor was still provincial. For example, it boasted a mere three balloons, and only one with a propeller. It was a small village, really, in an almost forgotten place, of interest primarily to those with an eye towards treasure hunting. Which didn't explain why Phinkerlington and his sister were in Luxor. Nor, of course, why Alessandro Tarabotti was.

"Catch a bite to eat later tonight, old man?"

Alessandro decided it was probably better for his image to be seen dining in the company of British tourists than to be observed too frequently about his own private business. "Certainly. But now, I'm afraid, I must beg to be excused. My man, you understand, is gadding about Egypt with a dead cat."

"Of course, of course."

Mr Tarabotti bowed to Miss Phinkerlington, who pinked once more at such direct attention. Not a bad-looking chit, really.

As he walked away, he heard the baronet say, in tones of deep censure and insufficient softness, "Really, Leticia, an Italian is most inappropriate. You must stop blushing at him so significantly."

Mr Tarabotti found Floote exactly where Floote ought to be – at the centre of a milling whirl of dark limbs and bright fabric, engaged in a protracted bout of fisticuffs. It was unsurprising that Floote, who had fought werewolves in Scotland and vampires all along the French Riviera, was holding his own. What was surprising was that he did this while still clutching the jar.

Alessandro removed his jacket and laid it atop a low mud-brick wall. He rested his hat carefully alongside. The jacket was tailored to perfection, flaring with just under enough fullness so as not to be thought dandified. It had three sets of invisible pockets in the lining, each housing a collection of sharp little sticks: silver, wood, and peppermint. The silver was for werewolves, the wood was for vampires, and the peppermint was for Mr Tarabotti. Mr Tarabotti was rather fond of peppermint. He was also fond of that jacket; it wouldn't do for it to be harmed, and he wouldn't need the weaponry, not in the middle of the day. He did transfer the letter of marque from the jacket to a waistcoat pocket next to his monocle and his miniature antikythera device, for extra security. Then he dove into the fray.

Alessandro was not burdened with Floote's sentimental British predilection towards proper violent comportment. When Mr Tarabotti fought, he used both his fists and his feet, drawing on a spate of skills he'd learned in the Orient. He would have been summarily thrown out of White's, for his technique was, it must be admitted, most ungentlemanly.

He enjoyed himself immensely.

Mr Tarabotti had always been fond of the occasional pugilistic endeavour, ever since he was a boy – revelling in that delicious slap and crush of flesh against flesh. He relished the heated blood buzzing through his brain, numbing all senses but those vital to security – sight and touch. Any pain was a boon, a reminder that he must keep his mind in play only so much as it did not hinder.

It was almost too easy. Floote's attackers were ill prepared for Mr Tarabotti's sudden appearance. Soon enough, the swirling mix of appendages and colourful flowing robes resolved itself into three local malcontents: one fallen and two running away.

While Floote recovered his equanimity, Mr Tarabotti sat astride the fallen man. He grabbed at the man's arms, pressing them to the ground.

"Who hired you?" he asked in English.

No response.

He repeated himself in Italian.

The man only looked up at him, dark eyes wide. He writhed about in the dirt, shaking his head frantically back and forth as though in the throes of some fit. Then, before Floote could put down the cat and render assistance, the man surged up, shook Alessandro off, and dashed away.

When Floote would have gone after him, his master stayed him with a touch. "No advantage in following. We won't extract any information from the likes of him – too frightened."

"Of us?"

"Of whoever paid them to engage the foreigner brandishing a dead cat."

"Hired by your contact, sir? Perhaps he changed his mind about notifying the government."

"No, no, I think not. There is someone else in play. Or several someones. Deuced inconvenient. Not to mention insulting. As if I would gad about town dressed like a manservant."

He went to retrieve his coat and hat.

"Who might be looking to stop you, sir?" Floote came over and straightened his master's lapels, checking the fit of the shoulders for good measure.

"Much good that blasted cat has done us. I thought it would provide quite the excuse for visiting Egypt. Now it's just making us easy to identify." The cat had caused quite the flutter at customs. Officials were used to dead animals being transported *out* of Egypt, usually of the mummy variety, but not *in*. Luckily for Mr Tarabotti's aunt, gold worked regardless of country, and Mr Tarabotti had the gold. The cat had served its purpose, until now. After all, why else would a rich Italian gentleman be travelling to Egypt during the high season of 1841?

"We must get rid of it, Floote."

Floote shifted his grip on the jar. "Shall I leave it in the street, sir?"

"Good God, no. Aunt Archangelica would never forgive me. Find someone to fix it up as she demanded, and quickly."

Very good, sir."

Sunset found Sir Percival Phinkerlington and Miss Phinkerlington awaiting Mr Tarabotti's presence at dinner in the hotel dining hall. Some crosses were meant to be borne during one's lifetime, Alessandro supposed. He joined them with a tight little smile, and helped himself to a glass from the mostly empty bottle of wine.

"Sandy, evening!" the baronet squawked.

Miss Phinkerlington blushed and nodded.

"Good Lord, man." Mr Tarabotti sipped the wine. It was cloyingly sweet. "Don't you own any other neckwear?"

The pleasantries disposed of, Mr Tarabotti settled back languidly in his chair, waiting for the first course of what, he had no doubt, would be an utterly unsatisfactory meal. "What happened to old Pink?" He was only half interested. "I thought he was due for the title, not you."

Out of the corner of his eye, he caught someone watching him closely from a nearby table. He leaned his chair back on two legs, tilting his head about in an attitude of foppish boredom. The watcher was a military gentleman of some breed, stiff about the neck and long about the hair. The man noticed Mr Tarabotti noticing him and returned to his food.

Sir Percival frowned, troubled by the Italian's bluntness. "You didn't hear?"

"Married beneath his station, did he? Go into trade? Die?" Alessandro tut-tutted, and declined to remark that society gossip had not been his focus during those few times he'd returned to England.

Miss Phinkerlington put a hand on her brother's arm. "Don't, Percy dear."

He patted her hand. "It's all right, Leticia. Sandy here's an old friend of Eustace's. Eustace always spoke highly of him. Played cricket together. Solid fellow." He leaned towards Alessandro, his breath redolent of cardamom and burnt aubergine. "Eustace tossed the title over. Gave it up to become claviger to some toothy old fluff of a lone werewolf."

"They always do take the smart ones from a family,

don't they?"

"Mother was devastated but, between you and me, it's probably for the best. Wouldn't have got any grandkids out of old Eustace. If you get my meaning." The baronet waggled his eyebrows.

Mr Tarabotti did. It also tickled his memory and explained why he'd visited the Phinkerlingtons all those years ago. Not an infiltration, as it turned out – at least, not an official one.

"Do I offer felicitations?" Mr Tarabotti sampled a rolled ball of some fried brown, crispy substance that in appearance resembled meat and in taste resembled sawdust.

"Only if he makes it through the bite and change. You understand how it goes. Oh, silly me, you don't, do you? Poor man. Italian." The baronet shook his head sadly – demonstrating the condescension of one country that had accepted the supernatural towards all the other poor, ignorant countries that hadn't. Open acceptance of vampires and werewolves was the thing that kept the British Isles separate from the rest of Europe. Well, that and their cuisine.

Alessandro stroked thoughtfully at the indent above his upper lip. "Ah, the English – confident in but two things."

"And what are those, Sandy my lad?"

"The supernatural and cricket."

Sir Percival laughed heartily, then stuffed his face with a number of the most uninviting-looking little cakes imaginable.

"You insulting the national pastime, old chap?" he said, fortunately after he swallowed.

"Which, the supernatural or cricket?"

"Cricket, of course. You used to bowl a nicely lethal over yourself, if memory serves. Spinner, no?"

"Pace bowler."

The baronet nodded. "Ah yes, I remember Eustace crowing about how fast you were."

Alessandro raised both eyebrows at that, but didn't reply. Out of the corner of his eye, he observed the blond military man stand up from his table and make his way towards the door, moving behind and around the various chairs in the dining hall with precise little twists. He disappeared, not upstairs to his rooms as one might expect, but out into the cold night.

"Fancy a little stroll, Phinkerlington?" suggested Mr Tarabotti, pushing his plate away petulantly.

The baronet, whose corpulence suggested he never fancied a stroll, little or otherwise, looked to his sister for salvation. She proved herself of no use whatsoever, a state evidently familiar to all around her, by saying, "Oh yes, Percy dear, do go. You know I don't mind. Some of the other ladies were planning on a game of bridge in the drawing room. I shall be perfectly entertained there until your return."

Sir Percival Phinkerlington's only possible excuse thus occupied with cards, the poor chap could do nothing but join Mr Tarabotti on his perambulation.

The hotel was situated near the northern edge of Luxor, the better to take in the view, such as it was: sand and dust on one side and the Nile on the other. They turned away from the verdant embankment, with its cultivated palm-groves, and headed towards the desert in all its burnt glory. A harvest moon hung low over two sets of limestone mountain ranges, one near and one far. Mr Tarabotti pulled out his antikythera and confirmed his suspicions – full.

"Crikey, that darn moon's bigger than a bison's bottom."

"Very poetical turn of phrase, Sir Percival." Mr Tarabotti put the antikythera away and searched the quiet streets. It was prayer time, so they were mostly deserted; yet he could not spot the missing military man.

They paused at the very edge of town. The baronet took out a large cigar, nipped the tip, and lit it with one of those newfangled aetherospark distributors. "Tell you the truth, old man, we're here for Leticia's health."

"Can't she withstand the damp?"

"No, not that. Hers is a health that's not quite right about the head, if you comprehend my meaning. Ever since Eustace went over. Chit sees night crawlers everywhere and wakes up screaming. Thought we'd bring her here." He puffed on his cigar.

"Because there are no supernatural creatures in Egypt?" Mr Tarabotti moved out of the smoke, coughing delicately. Cheap cigar.

"So they say, so they say. Like no snakes in Ireland. It's one of those things."

"True enough. There hasn't been a werewolf south of Alexandria in living memory." Alessandro thought of the papal letter of marque tucked securely in his waistcoat.

"Make a study of the supernatural, do you, Sandy?"

Mr Tarabotti said nothing.

"'Course you do. You Italians are all the same. Religious fanatics, the lot of you. Church says jump, you bounce about waving silver and wood, hoping it'll rid the world of all that goes chomp in the night."

"And yet I see acceptance of the supernatural has clearly done you and your family proud."

"Touché, touché. Fair enough. I'm not claiming to be a progressive, simply saying as how one extreme doesn't balance out the other. Far as I'm concerned, vampires and werewolves can do theirs, so long as I'm left alone to do mine. If you take my meaning." He removed the half-finished cigar from his mouth and looked at the glowing tip thoughtfully.

"Would you be so magnanimous, Sir Percival, had you not inherited a title because your brother chose the supernatural over family obligation?"

"Now see here, that's hardly the thing to say!"

Mr Tarabotti held up a hand sharply, cutting off any possible tirade. He cocked his dark head, listening.

Far away, somewhere in the depths of a desert wadi, something howled.

"Damn this country with all its foreign beasts. I'm telling you, it's all very well for Leticia's peace of mind – not a vampire in sight – but all these snakes and camels and jackals are playing hell with my finer feelings." Phinkerlington turned away, snorting.

Alessandro   frowned.   The   howl   came   again. "Werewolf."

The baronet tossed the butt-end of his cigar petulantly to the sandy ground. "That moon may be full, but don't be ridiculous. You just said, remember? There are no supernatural creatures in Egypt."

Floote was waiting for Mr Tarabotti in their rooms.

"Message, sir." He held out a little wooden tray with two crisp pieces of papyrus on top. Scribbled on the top one was a message in Italian, the tiny, messy script bleeding in places along the lines of the fibrous paper. Alessandro deciphered it while Floote divested him of his coat and hat.

"I'm to go there tonight. He apologizes for the skittish messenger this morning. Apparently, the boy was supposed to deliver this, but was spooked by our cat. Imagine being raised amongst mummies and fearing modern scientific preservation techniques." He switched to the second sheet of papyrus. "And a map. How very thoughtful. I wonder if that's what those bully-boys were after this afternoon? This map."

Lowering his hand, he raised an eyebrow at his manservant. "Speaking of the cat."

Floote pointed to a wobbly reed dresser upon which lay a smallish cat mummy.

"Is that...?"

"Not your aunt's feline, sir. The reports were perfectly correct; no one remembers how to mummify anymore. I found a willing apothecary, but the results were, regrettably..." A delicate pause. "Squishy. I managed to acquire that artefact, there, at a reasonable price and in excellent condition as a substitute."

Mr Tarabotti peered at the specimen through his monocle. "It'll have to do. We'll tell Aunt Archangelica they made it look emaciated and ancient for the sake of fashion."

Floote went to hang up his master's outerwear.

"Don't bother, Floote. I'll need it again immediately."

"Sir?"

"Tonight, remember?" He wiggled the papyrus with the map on it at his valet.

"Of course, sir, but surely not the gold coat? Most inappropriate for one of your evening engagements."

"Silly me. You packed the burgundy?"

Floote gave him a look that suggested he was gravely insulted that Mr Tarabotti should ever doubt such a thing.

The burgundy coat was a comparatively stylish affair, but cut looser than the gold to better hide multiple pockets, and with a full skirt to mask any additional accoutrement secreted about a gentleman's waist. Alessandro slipped it on while Floote bustled about putting various items on a large silver platter, which he then proffered politely to his master.

Mr Tarabotti selected from among the offerings, as a man will from a particularly delectable cheese plate: a nice bit of garrotte there, two vials of quality poison here, a tin of Germany's best phosphorus matches for extra zest, and a flask of turpentine to wash it all down. He chose one of the two pistols, the smallest and his personal favourite, checked that it was loaded, and stashed it inside a pocket over his left hip. After a pause to think, he took three cigars, the tidy little cheroots he preferred, and stashed them in the tin with the matches.

"Will you be requiring my company this evening, sir?"

"I shouldn't think so. After all, he is only an archaeologist."

Floote refrained from comment. He had spent over ten years as valet to Mr Tarabotti and, as yet, no one had turned out to be only anything. He smoothed down the sleeves of the burgundy coat and checked its armament carefully before buttoning it closed. He handed Mr Tarabotti a matching top hat.

"Will there be anything else, sir?"

Alessandro tightened his lips over his teeth in thought. "Perhaps the other gun as well, if you would be so kind?"

Floote passed it to him. "Try not to kill anyone important, sir."

Stashing the gun up his sleeve in a special quick-release wrist holster, Alessandro grinned. It was an expression that did not sit comfortably on his patrician face.

"Any final orders, sir?"

"The usual, Floote. If I don't come back ..."

"No record, no witnesses. I am aware of your standing instructions."

"Proceed then, Floote."

"Very good, sir."

There were more people in the streets when Mr Tarabotti exited the hotel a second time. Alessandro wondered if nightlife had evolved in Egypt due to the lack of supernaturals, much in the manner of peculiar animals evolving on islands without natural predators, if one were given to believe Mr Darwin's outlandish theories. Then again, perhaps it was simply the coolness of the air that encouraged wide-scale evening socialisation.

No one bothered him. No beggars whined for *baksheesh*. No tradesmen forced their goods in his direction. Alessandro Tarabotti had a way of walking that, even as a conspicuous foreigner in a foreign land, marked him as undesirable. Thus, he could move quickly through the narrow alleys that purported to be Luxor's main streets, passing whitewashed huts and undernourished obelisks, coming finally to a steep slope and sandy shore. Nearby, the three balloons were tied down, only one still inflated.

It took very little in the way of local currency or time
to hire a stunted raft, piloted by a lacklustre youngster, to
ferry him across the river. It took slightly more to
convince the urchin to wait. At two gold coins and
twenty minutes, Alessandro considered it quite
economical. The boat-boy even pointed out the path he
needed to take towards the tombs. Mr Tarabotti had paid
more for less in the past, and probably would again.

The map, it turned out, was not scaled as he might have
hoped, and it was a long walk of some four miles before
he noted any of the landmarks indicated there. He left
behind the lushness of the floodplain for a long limestone
canyon where litle grew and less thrived. He was grateful
for the moon, so that he need not carry one of the
ridiculous teapot-shaped oil lamps in order to see his
way.

It should have been a pleasant walk, but Mr Tarabotti,
whom no one would ever insult by calling anxious, could
not shake the feeling that he was being followed. Every
time he jerked about and looked behind him, he saw
nothing there. Nothing at all. This was compounded by
another sensation, one of being repelled, as though he
were a magnet too close to another of the same polarity.
He'd felt it ever since Cairo, but here it was worst of all,
almost unbearable.

He happened upon the archaeological encampment
eventually; a copse of canvas tents nestled at the base of
a cliff. It appeared quite deserted, so he clambered up to
the mouth of a rock-cut tomb, marked by an uninspired
X on his little map. As he climbed, a new scent overlaid
the clay musk of the cooling sands – tobacco and vanilla.

"I thought you hadn't received the message," said a
voice in Italian when he reached the top. A figure

resolved itself from gloom into a man by stepping forward out of the shadow of the rocks around the entranceway. Fragments of limestone crunched under sensible boots. "Trouble finding the place?"

"You sent a map. It had an *X* on it."

The man gripped Alessandro's shoulders, kissing him on each cheek in the manner of old friends. "Giuseppe Caviglia."

"Alessandro Tarabotti." Mr Tarabotti saw no harm in giving the archaeologist his name, though he objected to the intimacy of the rest of the greeting. "Show me what you found."

Mr Caviglia tilted his head to one side and took a draw on his pipe. "You know I can't simply do that."

Mr Tarabotti smiled tightly. "A rule player." He reached into his waistcoat pocket and pulled out the letter of marque, passing it over.

Giuseppe Caviglia unfolded and read it carefully by moonlight. "The government's full confidence? That must be nice."

"It has its benefits."

"You're authorised to take any action you deem necessary in conjunction with my findings here. What, exactly, does that mean?"

Alessandro ignored the question by asking one of his own. "You indicated in your original missive that this was a supernatural matter."

Mr Caviglia nodded once, sharply.

"Well, you caught the antiquities ministry's interest. They brought your letter to government oversight, and oversight brought it to the Templars, and the Templars brought it to me."

The archaeologist sucked in on his pipe sharply at that

revelation. Mr Tarabotti waited with ill-disguised impatience while Mr Caviglia coughed out puffs of vanilla-scented smoke.

Eyes watering, the man looked more closely at Alessandro's face. "You're one of them, aren't you? I thought they were all dead. Too susceptible to the poisonous humours."

Mr Tarabotti, who was in a bit of a poisonous humour, said sharply, "Interesting that you even know of my kind."

"My cousin is a Templar," Mr Caviglia explained hastily.

Alessandro grimaced. That could make things difficult.

Mr Caviglia recovered his equanimity. He handed back the letter of marque, openly evaluating his visitor's appearance. Alessandro knew what he saw: a man of lean build and patrician nose, tall, wearing a cleverly cut coat and trousers a little too tight. In short – a dandy. He would not see that the coat was cut to hide musculature, rather than exaggerate it, and that the tightness of the trousers was to distract from the smooth movements of the legs that wore them.

"You're not what I would have expected."

Alessandro cocked his head. "Well, at least one of us is surprised. You're exactly what I expected."

And the archaeologist was – unshaven, undersized, wearing round spectacles and a jacket no decent human would wish upon his worst enemy. He could be handsome under the grime, in a peevish scholarly way, but there were certain unforgivable flaws. Atop his head rested a battered object that might have started life as some species of hat many years ago and at the bottom of the ocean.

Mr Tarabotti shuddered. "Shall we go in now?"

Mr Caviglia nodded, tapping out his pipe on the side of the entrance. "A remarkable discovery, really quite remarkable." He led the way inside the tomb.

Its ceiling was higher than Alessandro had anticipated. A smoking torch in the far corner cast a dim, flickering light. It was as clean as could be expected of a place recently filled with rubble for thousands of years. There were few artefacts left – a broken column, several pottery bowls before an inset shrine, and a pile of digging tools nested at the base of the torch – but the walls were littered with carved and painted images. On one, a jackal-headed man sat at a vast banquet – bread, meat, and fruit laid out before him, a curly-tailed monkey crouched underneath his throne. On the other, the same man was shown undergoing various death rituals of a decidedly heathen nature.

"We found the tomb partly looted, of course. Most of them are. Oddly, the looters stopped halfway through and not a single person has touched the tomb since. Until we came along." The archaeologist crossed the room, grabbed up the torch, and led the way through a carved opening into a short passage.

Mr Tarabotti followed.

The passage turned to the left, and before them stood a huge basalt statue of a mummy, threatening and protective.

The archaeologist ignored this, turning again and leading the way down a steep set of stairs, talking all the while.

"Once we saw the mummy we realized why. The natives are terribly superstitious about these kinds of things. Well, you would be too, if you grew up in a land entirely devoid of supernatural. I mean, our government has been trying for elimination ever since the Inquisition, but the hives and packs will keep springing up. Not here, though."

Mr Tarabotti placed a hand against the tunnel wall to steady himself as he climbed down the dark stairs. "They're too strong and too well connected."

"Yet the Templars back home keep trying."

"They're believers." Mr Tarabotti grimaced as his hand came away from the wall filthy with dark brown dust and a fine yellow powder.

"And you?"

Alessandro shrugged. He believed in very little beyond his job and the wealth it generated.

"Well, regardless, this excavation has been fascinating. The sarcophagus has unique hieroglyphics on it. And the mummy – excellent preservation, stunning condition, from flesh to fibre. There."

They emerged into a room slightly smaller than the first, and far less tidy. It was cluttered, with antiquities spread across the floor and nestled into niches in the painted walls. Everything was covered in a thick layer of dust and, while some artefacts had been knocked over and broken, most were intact. The preservation was amazing. Wooden furniture stood in the corners, draped in crumbling textiles with large stone statues of animal-headed gods resting on top. Pots in every shape and size lined the walls, nestled amongst crowds of tiny human statues, piles of copper weapons, and a myriad of other mundanities. In the middle of the jumble, next to the massive hole it had obviously been hauled out of, stood a large sarcophagus of red granite, its lid off and tilted against its side.

The archaeologist tugged Mr Tarabotti over to it. Inside, a mummy lay partially unwrapped, the looters having started with its head, lusting after the precious amulets of gold and lapis tucked inside the linen bandages.

They'd stopped.

There was no doubt as to why.

"Remarkable," said Mr Tarabotti in English.

The creature inside was human, almost, but the bones of its face were not. Teeth, jaw, shape of forehead – all leaned more towards canine than man. There was even a light patterning of hair in the shrunken wrinkles of the dried brown skin.

"A werewolf."

"Undoubtedly."

"Mummified in half homo sapiens, half homo lupis form." Alessandro pulled a small analogue aether-omechanical transducer from his jacket pocket and prodded delicately at the mummy, testing for remnant vital aetheromagnetism. Nothing. "They say alpha werewolves can maintain just such a state as this, half in, half out of human form. They use it in metamorphosis rituals. Can you imagine?" His fine upper lip curled. "Disgusting." He investigated further. "Well, I commend you, Mr Caviglia. If this is a hoax, it is a very good one."

The archaeologist puffed up in outrage. "I assure you, sir—"

Mr Tarabotti held up the transducer autocratically to stop any denunciation and continued examining the body. "Don't you think that head shape is a little odd?"

"Aside from its being attached to a human body?"

"We call it *Anubis form*," said a new voice in old-fashioned Italian, flattened out by a British accent.

Out of the staircase entrance came the gleaming muzzle of a nasty double-barrelled pistol, followed by a blond military-looking gentleman.

"Hello, Curse-breaker," he said to Mr Tarabotti in English, gun steady.

"You were at dinner earlier this evening." Alessandro switched to the Queen's tongue, out of courtesy to their visitor, at the same time releasing his own gun out of its wrist holster. The movement was so subtle as to be imperceptible. The gun slid down towards his hand, almost peeking out of the bottom of one burgundy sleeve.

The man nodded. "I followed you from the hotel. As you inconvenienced me by not allowing my agents to steal the map from you."

Mr Caviglia raised both hands and straightened away from the sarcophagus. His eyes were fixed on the intruder's weapon.

Mr Tarabotti sniffed. "I knew someone was following me. How did I miss you?"

"You never looked up." The man had a soldier's bearing and a young face, but his eyes were dulled by past lives.

"I'm too old to remember humans have taken to the skies." Alessandro shook his head at himself.

"You're a werewolf," accused the archaeologist, with greater powers of deduction than Alessandro would have given him credit for.

The man snorted. "Not here, I'm bloody well not." He glared at Mr Tarabotti as though this fact were somehow his fault. "I hope you know what a bother it has been, travelling through Egypt after you these weeks. I had to learn to shave again, and every little cut takes a donkey's years to heal. I don't know how you mortals do it. I really don't. I hope you appreciate the risk I'm taking."

Alessandro licked his lips. This was going to be fun. "Oh, I appreciate it."

The un-werewolf narrowed his eyes. "Don't you move." He glanced briefly at the archaeologist. "Is it true what you found? What he said? Is that there a mummy of a werewolf in Anubis form?"

"See for yourself," suggested Mr Tarabotti, hoping the un-werewolf would come within striking distance.

The un-werewolf didn't take the bait, too old for that. "We used to rule this land. Did you know that?"

Mr Caviglia gave a little snort of disbelief.

"You archaeologists haven't figured that one out yet, have you? They worshipped us as gods. Turned sour on us in the end. Most things do. The god-breaker plague swept the Two Lands and, within a generation, every werewolf had died. We've not been back since, because this—" he gestured to himself, "—is what results."

"Mortality."

"And why would you risk everything to follow me here?"

The un-werewolf looked at Mr Tarabotti. "Curse-breaker, this mummy is our ancestor. You daylighters," and he included the archaeologist in his contempt, "have no right. Especially not some crusading religious fanatics. That mummy is the property of the British government. We have the concession, not the Italians. Ours to study and understand."

Mr Tarabotti smiled his tight little smile. "Who said we wanted to study it?"

The archaeologist and the un-werewolf both looked to him in shock.

"But the Templars promised."

Mr Tarabotti shrugged. "The Templars lied. And we can't very well have the English using this as some kind of pro-supernatural propaganda tool."

No record and no witnesses.

He slid the derringer smoothly the rest of the way out of his sleeve and into his hand, turned slightly in the same movement, and shot Mr Caviglia in the chest at point blank range. The archaeologist fell with a tiny cry of surprise and lay still against the corner of the sarcophagus, slumped and limp.

"We can't allow you to go babbling about this to the antiquarian community either, I'm afraid." He looked thoughtfully down at the scholar's dead body. "Pity."

The un-werewolf started, but his gun remained trained on Mr Tarabotti.

Alessandro tucked the now useless pistol into his pocket casually, feeling about for his second one, and narrowed his eyes at the man.

"What it must be like, seeing that—" he tilted his head at the fallen archaeologist, "—and knowing you could so easily end up the same way."

"Do you really think, after hundreds of years, we immortals fear death?"

"Do the crazy ones, who have lived too long, travel to Egypt to die voluntarily?"

The un-werewolf shrugged. "Some."

"So, we find ourselves at an impasse."

"Mmm, please take your hand out of your pocket, Curse-breaker."

Mr Tarabotti did so, tucking his second tiny gun up the end of his other sleeve in a manoeuvre he'd once learned from a street performer.

The un-werewolf gestured with his pistol for Mr Tarabotti to move away from the mummy and towards the door. Cautiously, Alessandro did so. But, near the entrance, as he passed close to his opponent, he pretended to stumble over a fallen urn, lurching violently to one side.

The un-werewolf growled at him and stepped threateningly forward.

Alessandro dove, shifting his weight and lashing up and out with his foot, striking the man's wrist where it held the gun.

The double barrel discharged a bullet, missing Mr Tarabotti by a foot, the slug ploughing hard into a support column, spitting limestone shards at both men. The un-werewolf swore and rotated the chamber to load his second shot.

Alessandro rolled, as much as he could, over the small statues and artefacts littering the floor, coming into a crouch covered in thousands of years of dust but with his second gun clutched in his hand.

He fired, hitting the un-werewolf in the shoulder. The shot wasn't deadly, but it did cause the man to drop his own gun in surprise.

Mr Tarabotti lunged for the fallen weapon at the same time as the un-werewolf, and the two of them scrabbled through the ancient offerings. Alessandro struck out viciously at his opponent, connecting where the shoulder wound seeped old blood, groping for the fallen gun with his other hand.

The un-werewolf backhanded Mr Tarabotti, handicapped with only one working arm, and that odd British distaste for kicking in a fight.

Mr Tarabotti had no such compunctions. Crawling as

they both were after the fallen weapon, Alessandro kicked out with one foot and managed to shove the man over. Grabbing the gun, he came up triumphant, pointing the weapon at the un-werewolf, who now crouched amongst the wreckage looking as savage as he might have in his lupine state.

Mr Tarabotti fired the last bullet. But the man was fast, even without supernatural speed, and managed to dodge. Frustrated, Alessandro threw the gun petulantly aside and pulled the flask of turpentine from his jacket.

He scattered it liberally about, making sure to coat the mummy in particular.

The un-werewolf lunged for him, seizing him by the waist and hurling him back to the floor. Mr Tarabotti pushed against the man's chin, trying to wrench his neck. His opponent howled, an animalistic sound coming from such a human face.

"That was you howling earlier this evening?" Mr Tarabotti panted out the question, clawing at the creature's eyes.

"Staying in practice, even if I can't change," came the hissed reply, as the un-werewolf struggled to hold Alessandro in a one-armed grip.

"That's rather perverse, you know that?" Mr Tarabotti uppercut sharply with the palm of one hand, achieving just enough leverage to break the un-werewolf's nose.

Alessandro squirmed away. Coming panting to his feet, he brushed off his burgundy coat with fierce, disgusted movements. "Is such dusty combat strictly necessary?"

The un-werewolf only bled at him.

Feeling deeply put upon, Mr Tarabotti reached once more inside his jacket, pulling out the tin of phosphorus matches. He backed away until he was at the doorway. There, he struck a match and threw it at the turpentine-covered mummy.

Seeing this action, the un-werewolf decided on self-preservation and charged past him up the steps.

The flammable liquid caught easily, the fire quickly spreading to burn away happily at the wooden furniture and textiles scattered about. From the amount of smoke and flames flaring up from within the sarcophagus, Alessandro had no doubt the mummy was ablaze as well. He whirled and ran up the stairs and out of the tomb, coughing delicately.

Outside, things were not as they should be. The un-werewolf was getting away, dangling precariously off the edge of the gondola of a hot-air balloon, floating upwards. A tubby sort of personage was manning the balloon's thermotransmitter and cranking up the hydrodine engine to get a steering propeller moving – a familiar tubby sort of personage, wearing a long scarf wrapped about his throat.

"Why, Sir Percival. I see you do own more than one item of neckwear."

"What ho, Mr Tarabotti? Sad business, this. I did so hope it wasn't you."

"Working for the Crown, are we, Phinkerlington? How menial."

"For the glory of the Empire, Mr Tarabotti. Can't expect a Templar's toady to understand, now, can I?" As he spoke, the baronet succeeded in getting the propeller in motion, and then waddled over to assist the un-werewolf in flopping, fishlike, into the safety of the gondola.

The balloon began to rise, its propeller whirling

mighty gusts of steam. Soon it would be at a height sufficient to set a steady course back to Luxor.

Alessandro flicked the air with the back of his hand, gesturing the men away as if they were mere irritations that had been bothering his evening's stroll.

No record and no witnesses.

He searched around his feet for a sharp fragment of limestone. The blaze from the lower part of the tomb had extended into the open room at the top. It lit the ridge-side on which he stood with flickering orange. It seemed the dust itself was flammable, and fresh air only encouraged the conflagration. He could hear the faint *poof* of limestone spalling in the heat.

He found a rock of adequate size. There was enough room on the hillside for him to run up his speed. Not exactly the perfect cricket pitch, but then, one couldn't be too picky about such things. Mr Tarabotti may have been born Italian, but he had bowled for New College, and been widely regarded as one of the fastest on record. The stone hit the balloon perfectly, tearing through the oiled canvas right above the engine feed, with immediate and catastrophic results.

The hot gas leaked out, deflating the balloon from one side and causing the whole contraption to list dramatically. The un-werewolf let out a howl of mixed anger and distress and Sir Percival swore, but there was nothing either man could do to salvage the situation. Moments later the balloon burst into flames, falling to the ground with a thudding crash.

Mr Tarabotti paused to light a cheroot with one of his remaining phosphorus matches and then walked towards the wreckage.

Both men were lying face down in the sand. Mr

Tarabotti turned the un-werewolf over with his foot, puffing softly. Definitely dead. Then he heard a small moan.

"Still alive, Phinkerlington?" He pulled out his garrotte and tossed the end of the cheroot away.

No record and no witnesses.

The fallen baronet turned his head weakly and looked at Mr Tarabotti.

"Looking less and less likely, Sandy my man," he croaked. "Nice bowl, by-the-by, perfectly aimed and you even got a bit of spin on it."

"I do what I can." Alessandro crouched over the fallen man and reached forward with the garrotte.

The baronet coughed, and blood leaked out the side of his mouth. "No need, Sandy old chap, no need. Do me a bit of a turn, would you? For old Eustace's sake, if not mine."

Mr Tarabotti sat back on his heels, surprised.

"See Leticia safely home to England, would you? Doesn't know dross about this business, I assure you. She's only a slip of a thing, good chit, really, can't have her wandering about Egypt on her lonesome. You understand?"

Mr Tarabotti considered. He'd have had to investigate the girl anyway. This gave him a good excuse to find out what she knew. He'd be terribly, terribly understanding and sympathetic. Tragic accident in the desert. What were they thinking, floating at night? He'd been out for a stroll and saw the balloon fall from afar. Dashed to the rescue but wasn't in time to save anyone. Old friend of the family, of course he'd be happy to escort her home.

Percival Phinkerlington's watery eyes bored into him. Alessandro pursed his lips and nodded curtly. The baronet sighed, closing his eyes. The sigh turned into a wet, rattling gurgle, and then silence.

Alessandro Tarabotti lit another small cheroot off the balloon's burning basket. What would he put in his report to the Templars? Such an incommodious bit of business. A dead un-werewolf was one thing, but a dead British aristocrat? He sighed, puffing out smoke. They'd not be pleased. Not pleased at all. And the mummy. Did his superiors need to know the truth of the mummy? For the truth was, that had been no wolf's head at all. Alessandro Tarabotti had killed enough werewolves to know the difference, emaciated or fully fleshed. No, it had been far more doglike, small, pointed. A jackal, perhaps?

He smoked his cigar. On the walls of that burning tomb, the jackal-headed god, Anubis, had been depicted assisting a jackal-headed man into the afterlife.

Werejackals? Surely not.

Alessandro snorted. But some twinge of fancy reminded him of the un-werewolf's words. *They worshipped us as gods.* And ancient Egyptian gods had other animal heads. Lots of other animal heads. No wonder the Templars wanted to keep such information out of British hands.

Mr Tarabotti turned to commence his long walk back to Luxor. Percival Phinkerlington, Baronet, might be dead, but Alessandro had to escort Miss Phinkerlington back to England and deal with a mess of paperwork as a result. He wondered which of them had got the better deal out of the arrangement.

Probably Phinkerlington.

AUTHOR'S NOTE

Thank you so much for reading *Romancing the Werewolf*. If you enjoyed it, or if you would like to read more about any of my characters, please say so in a review. I'm grateful for the time you take to do so.

I have a silly gossipy newsletter called the Monthly Chirrup. I promise: no spam, no fowl. (Well, maybe a little fowl and the occasional giveaway.) Join it on my website.

gailcarriger.com

ABOUT THE WRITERBEAST

New York Times bestselling author Gail Carriger writes to cope with being raised in obscurity by an expatriate Brit and an incurable curmudgeon. She escaped small-town life and inadvertently acquired several degrees in higher learning, a fondness for cephalopods, and a chronic tea habit. She then traveled the historic cities of Europe, subsisting entirely on biscuits secreted in her handbag. She resides in the Colonies, surrounded by fantastic shoes, where she insists on tea imported from London.